If I Die
Before I Wake

The Flu Epidemic Diary
of Fiona Macgregor

BY JEAN LITTLE

Scholastic Canada Ltd.

Toronto, Ontario,
1918

Saturday, August 3, 1918
My 12th birthday

Fanny and I came down the stairs together this morning and stood still in the dining room doorway while the family all sang "Happy Birthday" to us. Theo was too excited to stay on his chair but the rest waited for us to come and be hugged, which we did.

On my way down, though, I had been hoping against hope that I would not find another one of those little square diaries with skimpy square pages, all dated, wrapped up at my place. If I did, I was going to tell Father I refused to do it any longer, no matter how much my penmanship needs improvement.

Father gave Fanny and me our first two on our eighth birthday and told us to write in them every night before we went to sleep. When I was eight, I loved it. The pages were plenty big enough then, but after four years, filling in one of those squinched-up sheets every night with the weather and the tedious things I did became a boring CHORE. There was never enough room to record anything that really mattered. Now that we are turning twelve, I felt strong enough to mutiny.

When I faced the parcels piled at my place, though, I saw no square, diary-sized package. There were two that looked book-shaped but one was too small and the other much too big.

"You start first, Fee," Aunt said. "You are the older sister."

"Only by twelve minutes," Fan muttered.

Everyone but Jo ignored her. Jo, who was also born second, reached out and patted her hand comfortingly. "Everyone saves the best till last," she said.

Ha!

I pushed the parcels that looked like books to one side and opened the gifts from Jemma, Jo and Theo first. Jemma's was a box of watercolours, Jo's a sketch pad and drawing pencils and Theo's a box of sugared almonds, his favourite sweet. I said he could help himself and he grabbed a fat fistful before Aunt could stop him and crammed them all into his mouth. His cheeks bulged like a chipmunk's.

Everyone laughed.

Grandmother had not come downstairs yet so I had to go on to the gifts I had left unopened.

The smaller package turned out to be a copy of *Pride and Prejudice* by Jane Austen, with love from Aunt. I was pleased. I love to read.

But the card tucked under the ribbon on the second one read, *For Fiona Rose Macgregor, to record her 13th year, with love from her father.*

Father watched me read the words and laughed out loud. "Oh, Fee, you should see your face."

"You look as though you expect it to bite you or smell bad," Jemma said.

"I don't want to write in one of those diaries any longer," I burst out. I could not look at Father in case he was hurt, but I was determined.

"Open it before you decide. I think you just might like this one," he said.

Under the wrapping paper, I found this lovely book. It is much bigger than those others and it has a ribbon to mark my place. The paper is nicer, too. And the pages are not lined and dated but totally blank. They leave you free to write whatever you please. You can write one sentence or three pages. You can have a big life or a little one. What's more, you can skip days when there is nothing worth writing.

But I think I'll try not to skip.

Then, before I could speak, Aunt settled the thing. She said she wished I had known my mother better. "Ruth was so like you, Fee," she said. "She loved to write, too. If only our papa had made us keep a diary and you could read hers, you would find her to be a true kindred spirit."

I said all right, I would do it.

Fanny was not about to be skipped over. "How about me?" she asked. "It's my birthday, too, re-member."

"You are more like me," Aunt said. "You prefer deeds to words. You will notice you did not get a diary this year."

Fan had followed my lead and already opened a penny whistle from Jemma, the same paper and pencils from Jo and sticks of barley sugar from Theo. She put them in her pocket, out of his reach.

"You've had enough, piglet," she said.

Then she looked at her book-shaped package. Both of us had taken for granted that it was her diary. We so often are given identical gifts. But hers was a different shape. She tore off the wrapping and cheered up. It was a copy of *The Moffat Standard Canadian Cook Book*. Her card read, *For Francesca Ruth Macgregor, with which to practise making mouth-watering dishes for her family, with love from Father.*

Fanny beamed down at it. She looked like a simpleton. "I do love cooking," she said, "and I did hate writing in those little diaries every night. I made my writing scrawl to get it over with."

She jumped up and kissed Father. Why does she always have to beat me to it when it comes to being nice?

Then Father said we should get dressed and come outdoors to get our next present. I wanted to know what it was but Fanny ran for the stairs so I tore after her. When we came down, the front door was open and everybody but Grandmother was waiting in front of the house with our most totally surprising gift — a tandem bicycle!

"We are decidedly jealous," Jemma teased.

"We'll need to borrow it," Jo added. "Often."

Fan and I each have an old bicycle and have known how to ride since we turned nine. So we mastered the new one in about five minutes and took off, flying around the block and back. The best part is that we can hear what we say to each other as we speed along without needing to shout across a space. It has a basket on the back for holding sweaters or parcels.

Aunt got it second-hand from a woman who used to ride on it with her blind husband who died. She told Aunt that the bicycle would much enjoy being ridden by two young things.

Since we positively flew, I have named it Pegasus, the flying horse from the Greek myth. I love giving things just the right names. When we came back in, our little brother said, "You never ate breakfast."

Everyone laughed. I had not felt one bit hungry until then, but suddenly I was famished. Yet, even though I began to eat, I was still remembering what Aunt had said about my diary keeping.

Did she mean I like words better than deeds? If so, she is absolutely right. I would certainly rather read a book than peel a potato. Fanny, on the other hand, claims she actually enjoys household chores.

She loves baking and making things tidy. She told me once that she even likes ironing! And dusting!! She also said that polishing furniture was as satisfying as washing children's faces and dressing them up.

I don't like that job either. We are forever being told to tidy up Theo, who can get dirty just sitting still. I love my brother but I don't enjoy washing him.

Aunt is right about my longing to know more about my mother, too. Even if she had not died, how eagerly I would snatch up a book written by her when she was my age. She would probably put in all sorts of secrets, private things, her sorrows and her joys. I decided, then and there, that I would write this journal for the daughter I will have someday.

I told Father that I would make my new diary a letter to my daughter and he smiled and said, "You'll be writing more than one page a day, in that case. I'm glad I chose a larger book for you. Let me know when you are ready for Volume Two."

Fanny's second book was a manual of household hints. She started leafing through instantly, pleased as punch with the dullest stuff you could imagine. How to get coffee stains out of your skirt. How to get spruce gum out of a child's hair. How to make raspberry vinegar.

I had stopped listening to her when Father spoke to me in a quiet voice.

"After looking over what you wrote last year, Fee,

your aunt and I agreed that you needed more space to let your talent for writing flower. You must know you have a real gift," he said.

His words ran through my head like shining stars. *Let your talent for writing flower. . . . You have a real gift.*

Aunt agreed with him. I looked over at her and when our eyes met, she smiled and nodded. I decided, at that very moment, that they must believe I had actually shown some talent. I have never told them, but it is my dream to become a writer when I grow up.

One of my dreams anyway. I have others sometimes.

I could not think of a word to say back to them so I grabbed my Jane Austen book up to hide my face. I am afraid it looks a bit dull, not enough conversation. I hate books in which pages are a solid block of small print. Have you noticed, Daughter, that I am putting in conversation for you? Well, for myself, too. I did not like rereading my old diaries because I wrote everything on the page in one solid slab — except for the edge bits, which I stuck in later. I had to do it that way because each page was so small and you could only use one a day.

Back to the subject of Jane Austen's book, Aunt says Mother claimed she wanted to be just like Elizabeth Bennet, so I plan to read it and see what I think of E.

Later in the same morning

I can't believe how much I've written already. Reams! I wonder what a "ream" is. I wrote that much the minute I got up to Fan's and my room after breakfast. Then the postman came with cards for us. They were flowery and too gushy but they contained two one-dollar bills for each of us. They were from Father's old aunts who live out west. They have not seen us for years so it was really kind of them. I have stowed my riches away in my ribbon drawer.

I should tell about each of my family in here, one by one, so my daughter will know what everyone was like before she was born. It'll be like listing the Cast of Characters. I like books that start out that way, and plays, too. If I forget who somebody is, I can turn back and check. Not that I am likely to forget anyone in this book.

Cast of Characters

Father...........................David George Macgregor
Aunt.......................................Rose Mary Smithson
Grandmother..................Dorcas Joanna Macgregor
Jo...................................Josephine Mary Macgregor
Jemma.........................Jemima Amy Macgregor
Fee..Fiona Rose Macgregor
Fanny...........................Francesca Ruth Macgregor

Theo...........................Theodore David Macgregor
Pixie.........................Aunt's old Boston bull terrier

Those are the characters who live in our house, my immediate family members. I will leave other relations out unless they come into my story.

Until this minute, I never thought of my life as a story. I like the notion. I hope it is as good as *Pride and Prejudice*. Better even.

Describing Father is not easy. Telling what he looks like is simple enough, though. He has brown hair with grey bits at the sides. He has dark brown eyes. He wears glasses when he reads. He has a great smile although he does not smile over nothing. He has nice ears with a red pencil almost always behind one of them. He is six feet tall when he has his shoes on. He limps when he walks because he was injured in the Boer War and he uses a cane when he is tired and his leg troubles him. But the hard part comes when I think about his personality.

How much he has changed since Theo was born and Mother died! That was five years ago. I suppose we all changed at that time, but Father used to laugh so much more and tell us riddles and sing. He hardly ever does those things now. I know that he loves us as much as ever but he is more solemn.

Partly he broods about his friends who have gone to war while he could not go because of his limp.

I must try to get to know him better. He always has such piles of schoolwork to do, though, and so many meetings to attend now that he is head of the English Department. But I must not give up before I've even started.

I should go on and describe Aunt next but I need to think about her a while first.

After thinking and lunch

Grandmother gave us her present at lunch. It was a box of handkerchiefs with a flower embroidered in the corner. Fanny's was identical. Not only that, but they are the exact same handkerchiefs she gave us for Christmas last year. I wonder how many boxes she has stacked up waiting. We thanked her most politely but dared not look at each other in case we burst.

I must give you a name, Daughter, or you won't feel real. I will call you Jane in these pages. I just finished reading *Jane Eyre* and I like that name. It sounds plain and simple, just the way everyone thought Jane Eyre was, but she was not simple at all. She was brave and fiery and romantic. She stood up to lots of hardships. I am sure that you, Jane, will be like her.

Come to think of it, I believe maybe Aunt is like Jane Eyre — although she has never been in love as far as I know. Certainly she has never fallen head over heels in love with a man like Mr. Rochester. Are there any men like him? (There is some mystery about this but I will put that in later.)

She is not terribly tall. My older sisters are as tall as she. Her hair is nut brown. "The nut brown maids" they used to call Mother and her when they were young. She has very blue eyes and a grin that makes you grin back. I love her more than anyone, now Mother is gone. But she has a lot to bear raising all of us and standing up to Grandmother, and she does it just the way Jane Eyre would.

Jane was a teacher, and so was Aunt before she came to live with us. Years ago, she and Mother moved into Toronto to live with their aunt — right across the street from Father's house — while they finished high school. I bet they both thought he was wonderful.

If Grandmother were to read this, she would make me cross out *I bet*. She says betting is wicked. But she is not reading it and she never will if I can help it.

It was Mother he married. They were wed as soon as she graduated. Jemma and Jo were born two years later while he was away fighting in the Boer War. I'll tell about them later. That's when he was wounded and sent back to Canada. Aunt Rose came to help Mother nurse him and tend to the little girls. When he was well enough to go on with his teaching job, Aunt went to Normal School for a year and then left for a teaching job of her own in Alberta.

She came for Christmas most years but she never stayed long. I used to beg her to but she would just laugh. Until Theo was expected, that is. Things got too much then for Mother to manage, with only Myrtle Bridge to help. Myrtle still comes two mornings a week but she's slow. Father calls her The Weak Reed. Whenever he says this, Aunt shakes her head at him and says, "Myrtle may not be the sharpest knife in the drawer, but she does her best and I prize her above rubies."

Why am I going on about Myrtle? Well, I suppose I will be bound to mention her once in a while, Jane, and you would wonder who she was.

Mother wrote to Aunt and said she did not know how she could manage. Aunt packed her bag and came. I think my mother had a feeling something was wrong. When she guessed she might die, she asked Aunt to stay and raise her children. Aunt promised, and she has been here ever since.

Grandmother is next in the list. She will have to wait until later. We are going out to play croquet — even Father.

After croquet and a glorious birthday dinner

Jemma won the croquet game but she cheated. Jo accused her of nudging her ball into place with her toe. Jemma does not take such things to heart the way I might. She just laughed and said we were jealous of her tremendous skill.

Now to Grandmother!

I will confess to you, Jane, right off the bat, that she is not my favourite person. She has steely grey hair and steely grey eyes to match. Her nose is sharp and so is her voice. Her hands are hard. She wears spectacles all the time. She only laughs AT people and she smiles when she has been proved right about something.

She's mean. For instance, this afternoon she saw me curl up with *Pride and Prejudice* in Father's big leather chair and right away she called me to come and hold her wool for her. She could have asked Jemma or Jo, seeing it is my birthday, but not she. She had twelve skeins she had bought as a bargain and it took forever. Then she said, "Straighten up those shoulders, Fiona. If you slouch like that, you'll end up a hunchback."

I wanted to tell her my posture was none of her affair but I would be in very hot water if I ever dared speak my mind like that. I just shut my lips so tight they hurt and made my spine stiff as Father's walking stick.

Let's just say, Jane, that I liked Grandmother better when we just visited her. Now that she lives here, she is forever finding fault. Jemma thinks living with her was maybe what killed Grandfather off but I think that is going too far. In our family, Jemma is the one who is famous for going too far.

Our Smithson grandparents live together in their old farmhouse. They rent the fields to a neighbour now because Grandy is not strong enough to work them any longer. Jo gave him that name when she was small. It just fits him.

Grandma is not nearly as strict as Grandmother M. Grandmother even tries to boss Aunt around, though she is not a blood relation of Aunt's. Even Fanny thinks Grandmother is overstepping when she speaks to Aunt the way she does. After all, Mother and Father asked Aunt to come and live with us, but Grandmother just marched in. I should know. I saw it happen.

It's a long story but I'll tell it to you since Fanny is downstairs playing cribbage with Father and I just heard them start a new game.

It was a year ago, two days after Grandfather's funeral and I think they expected her to go on living in her own house with her maid. When she appeared at our front door with her portmanteau, I could see Father was taken aback, to put it mildly.

"I've put the house up for sale, David, and I'll be making my home with you in future," she said. Then she took a deep breath and went on. "I am correct in believing that you will be able to spare me a room in this big house of yours now that I am alone in the world, am I not?"

That is how she talks, Jane. I remember every word. Father looked as though he'd been struck by lightning. There was this loud silence. Then he answered her. "Of course, Mother. But what about Marta?"

Marta was her maid who had been with them for years.

"Marta handed in her notice the day after George died. She's gone to live with her sister in Orange-ville," Grandmother snapped. "You needn't worry about Marta."

"Well, Mother, you are welcome, of course, if you can stand living in this hurly-burly household. You should have sent me word and I would have come to fetch you. Fee, run and tell your aunt that your grandmother is here."

I thought he had forgotten I was there. He took her bag and led her into the sitting room while I ran to tell Aunt. She actually gasped, Jane, the way peo-ple do in books. She was sitting at the kitchen table shelling peas and she just sat and stared at me as though she couldn't believe her ears.

"He told her she can stay," I blurted out.

Aunt gave me the look I like least of her expres-sions. "What else could he do?" she said. "Would you have him turn his widowed mother away, Fee?"

I wanted to say yes but I knew better.

"She could have gone to Uncle Walter's," I said.

"Not if your Aunt Jessica had anything to say about it," Aunt said, getting up and going to get Grandmother's room ready.

She took over the spare room, the big one at the front of the house. It is big and bright and she has it to herself. She filled it with her own furniture.

We have never discussed it since, but when I told Fanny what had happened, sweet-tempered Fanny agreed with me that Father should have thought of his children and made some other arrangement.

I am probably crazy, Jane, but I think maybe my grandmother did not ask him ahead of time in case he said we had no room for her. Although Aunt is right. Father being Father, he couldn't have done such a thing.

To change the subject, did I tell you that Fanny and I are identical twins like Mother and Aunt? Aunt claims she can always tell us apart but it's not true. She gets it right when she goes by our expressions or how we behave. If you look at our noses or eyebrows or hair, though, we are the same. But not inside.

When I think something is funny, I grin. Fan claims it is unladylike to show your teeth. So she smiles with her lips closed. She thinks she is mysterious, like Mona Lisa. She looks ridiculous. Luckily she forgets a lot of the time.

And she is tidy. She really does have a place for everything and everything in its place. My untidiness is the cross she must bear, since we share a bedroom. I have tried to convince her that I am disorganized because I am far more creative than she and so cannot keep my mind on such petty details as the contents of bureau drawers.

"Balderdash!" she says.

We have brown hair that curls, especially when it is damp. We also have big, dark brown eyes. Theo, when he is being nice, says they are the colour of Father's coffee. (Father takes only a splash of milk.) Other times Theo calls them cows' eyes.

As I have said, Fan is sweet-natured. I, on the other hand, am often grouchy or I lose my temper completely and fly off the handle. What "handle" do you suppose that is, Jane? It is an odd expression. I relish odd expressions.

I do love Fan, Jane. She is my twin and I cannot imagine life without her. But we are NOT the same kind of person. I sometimes think we are not as close as twins are supposed to be and that I care more for my older sister Jo. But I am not sure about this.

Father and Fanny must be playing ANOTHER game of crib. That means she won and so he has to show her he is still better at it.

Aunt made us a scrumptious lemon sponge cake for our birthday. I love sponge cake but we have not had it for ages because of the War. Aunt saved up extra eggs and sugar for it. I was so generous I slipped Pixie a bite. She smacked her lips so loudly I was afraid Grandmother would hear, but she didn't.

I got the ten-cent piece in the cake, which means I will be rich. Theo got the button, which means he won't get married this year. Lucky thing, since he is not six yet.

Jane, your Aunt Fan is here at last. So, my dear daughter, I must put out the light and leap into the bed before my sister falls asleep and lets her big knobbly feet slide over into my half. Her toenails scratch.

Good night.

Sunday, August 4, 1918

I promised to tell you about Jo and Jemma later and I will begin today's entry by keeping that promise.

Jemima and Josephine, called Jemma and Jo for short, are twins, too, except Jemma was born ten minutes before midnight and Jo came along just after the clock stopped striking. So they have different birthdays. They are fraternal twins, which means they are not identical. It is strange because *frater* means "brother" in Latin. Brothers they are not.

They just turned eighteen. Nobody has trouble

telling those two apart. Jo is much smaller and browner while Jemma is fair and willowy. That's Aunt's word. I would have said lanky or skinny. But Jemma would rather be "willowy," I am sure.

They both just finished Fifth Form and Jemma is planning to become a teacher. She wants to have a class of infants. She says your first years of schooling are the ones that matter most.

Jo, if she can wear Father down, wants to be a doctor. He says girls are meant to be nurses, like Florence Nightingale, but Jo brought a girl home from Sunday School — she is in the senior girls class that Miss Banks teaches — who is going into Meds in September even though she is only sixteen. She is awfully nice. She talks to me and Fanny as if we are the same age as she is. Her name is Caroline Galt. I guess it was their both wanting to be doctors that made them strike up a friendship. By now, you would think they had known each other for years instead of only a few weeks. I wonder if Jemma is jealous sometimes. I would be if Fan began to chum around that way with another girl. We have separate friends, of course, but we are still closest to each other, in spite of what I said earlier. Jo and Jemma have always been that way too.

But Jemma does not seem jealous. She appears to like Caroline almost as much as Jo does. And she has Phyllis Trent and Nancy Spry to chum around with.

Nancy wants to be a teacher too, although she wants to teach older children. She is a loud, jolly sort of girl whom children will like, I think. They'd like Jemma too. When she is with little children, she is gentle. When she isn't, she's flighty and much funnier and more dramatic than Jo. Phyllis means to stay at home and help her mother until she gets married.

Caroline Galt is called Carrie by her brothers and sisters and Caroline by her parents. She got her Matric out west where you only have four years of high school, not five years, like here. Her father went with her to sign her up at the university, and persuaded them to let her start in September. I guess they couldn't say no to a missionary minister.

About Jo though, I think talking to Caroline and her dad has made Father weaken. He has given Jo permission to go into medical school this fall if it is not too late for her to register. Aunt is on Jo's side, of course. She thinks it would be good for Jo to have Carrie to chum around with. They don't want her making the wrong sort of friends. Carrie, being a missionary's daughter, is made to order. I think they are foolish to fret about this. As if Jo would be chums with a "bad influence."

Jemma's the one they should be worried about. When Fan and I were taking a last spin on our tandem before we came inside, we saw her a couple of blocks from home with three boys, and she was making eyes at all of them and laughing a flirty laugh. When we got home, she asked us to keep mum about the boys and we said we would. You wouldn't catch Jo behaving like that.

I will back up now and tell more about the Macgregor family.

I already told you about Grandmother. I suppose Father must love her. She is his mother after all. But they don't seem close. She likes cooing at tiny babies — but not changing their nappies. She likes well-behaved small children. She likes playing peek-a-boo and waving bye-bye. She used to dote on Theo. But when he grew bigger and sassy, he stopped being her pet. When she speaks of him these days, she calls him "the boy" and sniffs.

I think I said already that she got the front bed-room. Everybody else, except Father, has to share. Theodore slept in Father's room until he started having nightmares. When you have a nightmare, Father is useless. When Theo kept waking up screaming and Father could not comfort him, the clever boy marched into Aunt's room and climbed in with her. Father moved his crib in and Theo has never gone back.

I already told you about Aunt too but I left out some important things. I cannot understand why she has never married. I put this question to Mother once and she gave me a queer look and said, "Don't ask,

Fee. It is private. And it is not her fault but mine."

I asked what she meant, of course, but she would not explain. She told me instead that it was not my business and to forget what she had said. It was strange. She did not sound like herself. I have forgotten so much since she died, but those few puzzling words stuck in my memory like a cocklebur. Have you ever noticed, Jane, that the minute somebody tells you to forget something, it becomes impossible? My mind, anyway, grips the bit of whatever it is all the tighter. This is especially true if there is something mysterious about it.

The older I get, the more I wonder what she meant.

It was as though she almost told me a secret and then changed her mind, deciding I was too young to be trusted. Well, I was only seven. I've always had trouble keeping secrets. But I'm not seven now. I have almost decided to try to ferret out the truth. I can't believe Mother would mind my knowing after all this time. But I can't ask Aunt herself. Mother made that plain.

Fan and I were born six years later than the Almost Twins. When we were seven and Jo and Jemma were thirteen, Theodore came along.

Mother died just three days later. I don't know why except that she was sick beforehand and "burning up with fever" afterwards and they "could not stop her bleeding." Nobody told me this, of course. They don't tell children such things. But I overheard Aunt talking to one of her friends about it.

It is almost enough to make you decide not to have children, except there are so many mothers around who have their first baby and then go right ahead and have more without seeming the least bit worried. It is a puzzle.

Bedtime

We went for one last ride on our tandem after supper. People turned and pointed at us. It is such a perfect present for twin sisters. Today is windy, too, and I loved feeling my hair lifting off the back of my neck and blowing out behind me. I wanted to sing so I started in on "A Bicycle Built for Two." Fan was shocked for a second and then joined in. She always has to decide whether or not she is being ladylike. I know I am not ladylike so I don't have to bother thinking about this.

Writing the diary this way makes it easy to pick up and put down. It is like talking to an invisible chum. Someday, Jane, you will stop being invisible and that will be lovely even though I will have to grow up before we meet in the flesh. You will be relieved to hear that I do like babies.

Theo believes Aunt is his mother. He keeps calling her Mama and she has almost given up correcting him. It sounds right. After all, he never knew Mother the way the rest of us did. To him, Mother is like someone in a story. Aunt and Theo are Mama Bear and Baby Bear, I think. I will confess to you, Jane, that it sometimes feels as though Aunt is my mother too, though I would never say so out loud.

I remember our real mother singing us to sleep. I can still hear her soft voice singing "Lullaby and good night" and "Sleep, my child, and peace attend thee, all through the night." I was afraid of the dark back then and she knew it. She left a light on to comfort me. She smelled like flowers. At first, after she died, I used to go into her closet and smell her dresses and it seemed as if she were still there. Then, one day, they were gone and I cried but couldn't tell Father why.

But now, if I try to call up her face on purpose, it blurs and I cannot hold onto it. I have to depend on quick glimpses my memory gives me.

After she had Theo, she held him up for Father to behold and announced, "At last, David, I have given you a son."

I can see her laughing face then. And hear his voice answering.

"You make me sound like Henry the Eighth," he said. (Later on, in History class, I learned that Jane

Seymour was Henry VIII's wife and the mother of his only son.)

It is high time I told you about Theo properly. You'd think we girls would hate our baby brother, but he is the one thing everybody in our household agrees about. He is a darling. Most of the time. He has a mop of fair curls, enormous blue eyes and a smile that would melt the heart of an ogre. I think the blue of his eyes is the colour of chicory flowers. He is just plain nice. I heard Aunt call him "quaint" once and that is true too — if I am right about what "quaint" means.

I can't believe I have already written such volumes in this diary. Never before have I let my pen run away with me like this.

One thing I haven't mentioned, though, is that our country is at war. You would think I would have put that on the first page. But the news is always so terrible and the fighting seems far away mostly. I heard this afternoon though that Calvin Anderson was killed in the fighting. His younger sister Prudence is in my class at Jesse Ketchum. I don't know her well and I don't like her much. She's too prim and preachy. A real goody two-shoes! But tonight she must be heartbroken and I feel sorry I don't like her better.

Father still thinks the War must end before long. But I have been hearing that for years and years, and it is still going on. It started just a week before my eighth birthday. Theo has never lived in a world at peace!

Father just looked in and asked me if I had written my thoughts on this morning's sermon in my journal. He is teasing, Jane, because I laughed out loud in church. It is too long a story to tell now but I will tell you in the morning. My hand feels stiff from writing so much.

Monday, August 5, 1918

Here is the story. I was sitting in the pew watching Theo. He had quietly produced a tiny toad from his pocket and was playing with it. While I was spying on him out of the corner of my eye, it got away from him and jumped right into Mrs. Barber's enormous black purse which she had opened to get out her handkerchief just as the minister started on the long prayer, the one where you ask God to bless the king and everybody. It is even longer now, what with praying for the troops and victory. She did not notice the toad because she had her eyes shut, of course.

I hardly ever shut mine because my keeping them open annoys Grandmother. She says you have to shut your eyes, bow your head and fold your hands to pray properly. I asked Father about this and he said the Almighty cared about your prayer, not your posture.

The toad did not reappear and I suddenly thought of it jumping back out and leaping onto the collection plate when she got out her offering. Can you blame me for giggling??

At lunch yesterday Aunt asked me what was so funny, but I could not tattle on Theo so I just said it was a private joke. Father shook his head at me and Theo shot me a look of pure thanksgiving.

Grandmother says I should pray for strength to resist the sin of levity. She did not see the toad. I don't think the minister even noticed my laughing. He went right on praying for the whole world, person by person.

See you later, Jane. Fanny wants to go for yet another spin around the neighbourhood on Pegasus and show him off again. I am happy to oblige.

Bedtime

I forgot to say that Carrie Galt and Miss Banks came in after Sunday School yesterday and heard Fanny singing. She does have a lovely voice. Aunt says she gets it from Mother. Aunt and I have deeper voices that are sort of husky. That is one way Fan and I are not identical.

Because of Fan sounding like a lark, Miss Banks

has invited all four of us to go along with them to sing to some of the wounded veterans in the hospital. They have not told us the date we do this. It has to be arranged. I feel scared inside but I don't think it showed. I hope we don't see anyone actually suffering or have to hear moaning or screams.

I wonder if Fanny is nervous, too. You would never guess it from looking at her face, calm as a mill pond.

I wonder what is so calm about a mill pond. Mill ponds must get ruffled on windy days. Wouldn't "calm as a cabbage" be better? Cabbages stay placid even during slam-bang thunderstorms.

Maybe Fan would dislike being compared to a cabbage though. How about a vegetable marrow? No. "Calm as a sleeping baby." Good. She'd like that.

Placid as a pudding?

Tuesday, August 6, 1918

This morning, Aunt announced it was cod liver oil day. The doctor who told Aunt to force every one of us to swallow a walloping great spoonful of the disgusting stuff every week, and to drink a glass of orange juice and castor oil once a month, should be shot. I told Fan what I thought. Gentle Fanny Macgregor, famous for her kind heart, said, "Being shot is too kind. He should be boiled alive in cod liver oil after having been forced to drink a gallon of castor oil." I was shocked!!

We did not know Theo was sitting under the table until his little voice floated up to us, sounding so serious. "Off with his head! That would be best," he said.

After supper

Jane, we have a dog! We have begged for a dog for YEARS. Always we were told not to be so silly. "We have a dog," Father would say, pointing at Pixie.

Pixie is definitely a dog. She is Aunt's Boston bull terrier. She came here when Aunt did, just before Theo was born. She was already eleven years old. Now she is sixteen. And although we are fond of her, she loves only Aunt. She is black and white and she must have been a cute little pup once upon a time. She is so old now, that every breath she takes wheezes as though she has asthma. She doesn't want to play with any of us but only hobbles around on her spindly bow legs after Aunt. When her mistress sits down, Pixie gives a great sigh and thumps to the floor to catch a nap before Aunt rises, forcing her to move again. If Aunt goes too fast, Pixie sounds as though she is breathing her last. She is not an enjoyable pet.

But today we got a real dog and it is so astounding. The doctor did it. He dropped in to see Theo, who has had a worrying cough. While he was here, he told us about one of his patients who has died and left a dog without an owner.

"He's housebroken, his sister says, and he's a great dog," Dr. Musgrave told us, "but I can't keep him. I'm out too much. Would the children be interested? All he does is grieve and I am worried about him."

I asked what his name was because I am fascinated by names. The doctor said nobody knows. The man just called him "Dog" as though that was a name. I think that is shameful. I wonder how he would like to be called "Man" or "Person."

"Please, Daddy," Theo said, opening his eyes wide and looking like a heartbroken angel. "Please. I've yearned for a dog for so many long years."

We could not help laughing at him. But Father said to bring "the animal" over and we'll have a look at him before deciding.

"Right now," Theo begged and then asked to go along for the ride so he could hold the puppy. The doctor burst out laughing. When he and Theo returned, I understood that laugh.

Our new dog came thundering through the door like a baby elephant, Jane. Theo had his arms flung around as much of his neck as he could hold. And he was being dragged along on his tiptoes.

"Welcome, Hamlet, Prince of Denmark," Father said, laughing and then bowing low.

Hamlet is a Great Dane and he is ENORMOUS. We all adore him. I don't know if Father would have kept him if he had not been inspired by the thought of a Great Dane named Hamlet. Naming someone connects you to whoever you name.

Aunt choked down a shriek, but when Pixie wagged her unimpressive tail end madly and let herself be sniffed "from stem to stern," as Father said, darling Auntie came around. I think it was our lucky day that Grandmother had gone to her WCTU meeting. By the time she came home, Hamlet was a member of the family and she had to like it or lump it. All she could think of to say was that we could not afford to feed such a brute. Theo instantly offered to do without half his food for the monster's sake. (Theo is a picky eater. Poor Hamlet would be nothing but a bundle of bones if he had to live on just half of Theo's meals.)

"Jim Swenson will let me have all the tripe this fellow can eat," Father said. "He'd never have passed his final exams if I hadn't coached him."

Jim S. is the butcher's son. Tripe is disgusting. It's the lining of the cow's stomach or something. Aunt tried to cook it for us once but nobody could choke down even one bite. It's white and slimy. Hamlet won't mind though. He looks big enough to eat the whole cow. When Father went and fetched some tripe home, Hamlet's tail whipped back and forth with enormous enthusiasm.

The dog's name is Hamlet, Jane, because Hamlet, in Shakespeare, is a Danish prince. Father had to explain to everyone but me. I had read it one rainy afternoon. It is in a book with Mother's name on the flyleaf.

When Hamlet is standing up, Pixie walks under him as though he is a table or a bridge. He peers down at her and wags his long tail happily.

Wednesday, August 7, 1918

Oh, Jane, you should have seen Myrtle when she laid eyes on Hamlet. You know how Lot's wife, in the Bible, was turned to salt? That's how poor Myrtle looked. But Hamlet just went over to her and kissed her fingers and, with only one small shriek, she came around.

I had a busy day, Jane, what with petting Hamlet and making jam. I admit to you and you alone, that for every raspberry I put in the bowl, I ate two. Aunt finally told Fan to take my place and ordered me to get busy and finish the ironing, which should have been done yesterday. Myrtle was here so she could have done it. I detest ironing. Aunt knows this full well.

I finally got a break by agreeing to play catch with Theo. Whatever Theo wants, Theo gets!

Thursday, August 8, 1918

Another day of making jam. Peach this time. We were short of sugar but the peaches are wonderfully sweet. And we have to do more canning tomorrow. I'll write again when it is done. I hate doing the canning, but all the jars, lined up, look beautiful. Like tall, fat jewels with silvery hats.

Friday, August 9, 1918

Father came home early with the newspaper. He looked grim. We were all laughing and the sight of him made us feel guilty, as though we'd been making fun while our men died in the trenches. He said he still thinks the War will be over before Christmas. It has been going on forever and it just seems normal most of the time. Then something will happen, like seeing wounded soldiers at the train station or hearing Father talking about men he knew who died at the Somme or on Vimy Ridge, and it is so real it is frightening. I am lucky I have no brothers at the Front.

Carrie Galt's brother Gord was killed last March. When his name is mentioned, the War is suddenly terribly near and real. I think of it and my heart aches for all the young men. Yet, half an hour later, I will be dithering over what to wear to the Sunday School picnic and the War will fade into the distance again. Aunt says our minds work that way to protect us from more horror than we can face. She is probably right.

After Father went into his study, we crept about until Hamlet started chasing Pixie. Old as she is, she dances out of his way while he trips over his clodhopper paws. It is such fun to watch them.

Hamlet helps with all the worry about the War. He is such a solemn dog that he has us in stitches, like a sad clown. He also keeps trying to climb on our laps and jump on the beds. They, and we too, collapse. Aunt is making us keep the bedroom doors closed. We are not to allow him up on the sofa, but he stares at it so sadly.

"If that creature jumps up on my bed," Grandmother said, glaring at him, "he or I will leave this house."

The Danish Prince backed away from her at once and tucked his tail between his legs. He understands her meaning so well that he does not even go to her door. She has a powerful glare.

I saw Theo's lips part and knew, by the fire in his eye, that he was about to say that Grandmother would have to be the one to go because Hamlet was staying no matter what. I stepped up behind him and put my hand over his mouth. "Don't," I warned him.

He shook my hand away but kept his lips sealed.

Aunt found an old plaid steamer rug with a fringe for Hamlet to lie on. He likes it so much that he drags it with him from place to place and then gazes at us mournfully until somebody lays it flat for him to stretch out upon. He and his rug take up a LOT of floor space. If the fringe is standing up when he puts the rug down, he lies and blows on it. Theo says he is not trying to flatten it, he just likes to see it wave. Theo spends hours talking with him, so he should know.

If Aunt is busy in the kitchen and has no time to sit down and make a lap for Pixie, her dog goes and leans against Hamlet as though he is a sofa. They look so comical! Then they soon launch into a snore duet! Even Myrtle, who is mostly silent and sober, smiles ever so slightly.

I warned my little brother not to try tempting Hamlet up on Grandmother's bed. He stared at me with shocked eyes.

"As if I would," he said in a perfect imitation of Aunt.

Saturday, August 10, 1918

Word came today of a big battle at Amiens. We don't know the details because it only happened yesterday, but Father has somehow learned that there were many men killed. Our troops made a twelve-mile advance, which is supposed to be terrific. But I think many men dying only to win twelve miles of earth seems wicked. Father told me that this could well be the beginning of the end. I don't know why God can't stop it. I told Jo that and she just shrugged and said, "God didn't start the War, Fee. We did." I wanted to yell at her, "Not me!" But I did not. She had been crying. She's afraid one of the boys who joined up at the end of the school year may be among the dead. I don't think it is possible. How could they have gotten over there that fast?

I was getting into bed when I heard Aunt starting to play the piano softly. She used to play much more before Grandmother came but, whenever Father is especially troubled, she will go quietly and play for an hour or so. It helps us all. Once, when she began, I saw Grandmother's bedroom door open. I told Aunt and she smiled.

Sunday, August 11, 1918

This morning, on our way to church, my hat blew off. I chased it down the road only to find it in the street with a great lummox of a horse standing on the ribbon. The man who owned the animal had gone into a nearby house for some reason and did not see. The horse did move on at last, and let the hat blow into the gutter, where I rescued it. But it definitely needs a new ribbon. Maybe I'll use my birthday money and buy yards of ribbon. At the drygoods store, you can get a yard of satin or moire ribbon for 25¢.

Saturday, August 17, 1918

Last Monday evening, our Aunt Jessica, who is Uncle Walter's wife, arrived out of the blue and invited Fan and myself to come home with her for a week's visit. I was surprised, because she never used to invite us and now she has asked us twice. I told Jo I was surprised and she said she suspected that Aunt Jess knows she ought to have Grandmother visit and give Aunt a vacation from her, but she cannot bring herself to do it. So she asks us instead. I wonder if Jo is right.

In the excitement of packing, Jane, I forgot this book and left it hidden away at the back of the book-case where I keep it safe from prying eyes. I did take *Pride and Prejudice*. It is a bit slow going but I do understand why Mother liked Elizabeth Bennet. The younger sisters are tiresome. Jane is nice though. She reminds me of Fan a little.

We had a pretty good time. Uncle Walter is away at his drugstore all day so we don't see much of him, but he isn't a relaxed sort of man anyway. They live out of the city but near Sunnyside, within walking distance of Lake Ontario and, freezing cold as it always is, we went swimming every day even though we turned blue and got covered with goosebumps. I wish someone would invent a material to make bathing dresses less clammy. Wet wool is highly unpleasant. But it was worth it. We would sit on the beach at sunset and watch the stars beginning to come out over the water.

Our cousins were away visiting Aunt Jessica's parents in the States so we did not have to put up with their bossy ways, which was nice. They are both boys. They are fifteen and eighteen and they think they are in command of everyone younger. They order us around as though we were their personal slaves. They are rough, too. When their mother is not looking, Tom will grab your arm and twist it or George will sneak up on you and smack your back hard enough to make you stagger. Then they laugh like hyenas.

Maybe Aunt Jessica sees more than we think and that was why we were invited while they were away.

Even though I enjoyed myself, I was pleased to get home to Theo, who could not come because of his sniffles, and to Hamlet, who almost knocked us flat with his exuberant welcome. You have to dodge his tail when he gets excited. It is strong enough to sweep all the cups and saucers off a tea table. Aunt says it is his way of smiling and she puts the china out of tail's reach.

Jo and Jemma took Pegasus out for regular outings so he did not pine. Ha! We'll have to watch it or we'll lose our trusty steed.

We go to sing to the soldiers tomorrow afternoon, Jane. Wish me luck — and courage. I wish I could take Hamlet along. He would cheer even the most sorrowful soldier.

Sunday, August 18, 1918

We are home from the hospital and Fanny is asleep so I have stolen out of our room and I am writing this in the hammock on the front verandah. It may make my writing a bit like a range of mountains for it sways every so often and my pen slides up and down.

What a time we had at the hospital! We all dressed alike in middies and dark skirts so we looked like a choir. We did see some sad things. The worst one, for me, was a man who looked fine at first glance but never smiled or spoke or moved. He has lost his sight and his memory from "shock following a head wound." The wound has healed now but he just lies and does not speak. I did see him blink but never once did his eyes move or seem to be seeing anything. Imagine not seeing the world around you and not knowing who you are or even where.

They lined us up and I was put right next to his bed. I could easily have reached out and taken his hand. It lay there on top of the coverlet and never moved at all. It made me shrink up small inside, being so close to such loneliness. I wanted to pick up his poor hand. But I didn't dare.

Something comical happened though, near the end. We were all singing "Steal Away" and Fanny had just sung, by herself, "Steal away, steal away home. Steal away to Jesus . . . " when a fat man with a bushy red beard and a bald head and only one leg snatched up a crutch which was standing next to him and waved it over his head. "You do it, my sweet girlie," he roared out. "You steal off to Him. You couldn't steal away to a better place."

Then he made the men all clap for us and a couple of the others cheered and the whole bunch began to laugh and joke in a way Grandmother would call "brazen" or "demented." The nurse told us she thought we had sung beautifully but perhaps we should leave now before things got out of hand.

We began to go and the men called to us to come back soon and to behave ourselves and a great mix of teasing things.

"Don't do anything I wouldn't do," one shouted right at me.

He had bandages everywhere and one of his friends roared, "Poor kid. YOU can't do a thing he hasn't tried." Another said, "Don't you listen to him, sister." I tried to see if the blind one smiled but I couldn't because by then his bed was in shadow.

Just thinking about their courage, laughing like that when they were suffering so, makes me so sad. Fan was sobbing before she fell asleep.

I hope, when you are my age, Jane, that there are no more wars in the world and nobody ends up in a ward like that. This war is supposed to be the last, but Father says anyone who believes that is no student of history or human nature. Aunt calls him a pessimist. Perhaps I AM getting to know him better. I don't think he is a pessimist. He is a man with a heart breaking over the suffering he reads about.

One of Jo's class was killed at Amiens, just as she feared. He was a tall, handsome boy with curly hair and dancing brown eyes. He never saw me, of course, but I think he liked Jo. She and Jemma went to the station to see the boys off when they left. I asked to go along but they would not take me.

"It is no place for children," Jemma's snooty friend Pam said in her drawly voice. She thinks she sounds like an actress. I am sure Jo thinks she is silly but Jemma admires her because she is so "sophisticated." Jemma thinks she is beautifully slim. She's really a positive beanpole with hips like doorknobs.

Jo is grieving for all of the soldiers who are overseas. At first — years ago now — we all thought they were so handsome in their uniforms, and the band music made you feel proud and excited. The flags flying and the band music and the uniforms stir your heart. But by now everyone has seen wounded men like the ones we sing to or men who suffer from shell shock. Some people say the shell-shocked men are really just cowards and they are pretending to be ill so they need not go back to the Front. I would not blame them if it were true, but Father says such people show their ignorance and their utter lack of compassion. He can hardly speak because he is so angry.

One of his friends came back like that and Father spends what time he can spare visiting him. They used to play chess but now the man's hands shake too much.

Aunt played the piano until after eleven tonight. Now she has stopped, I will be able to go to sleep. Father too.

Monday, August 19, 1918

I spent a whole dollar on four lengths of ribbon, all gorgeous colours. Too bright for my hat? No siree! I intend to cut a dash with them wound around the brim or dangling down my back. I bought extra because you never know when a horse will tread on your hat ribbons. Grandmother says I am wasteful but Aunt stroked the satin ribbons as though she'd like to steal one or two when my back was turned.

Something odd happened at supper. Grandmother suddenly remarked, in a loud voice, "I saw Dulcie Trimmer today." I've never heard of anybody by that name but Grandmother was staring at Father as though he knew who she meant. There was a funny silence and then he said, "Oh. How is she? I haven't heard of her in years."

"As pretty and friendly as ever," Grandmother told him. "She gave up her job as headmistress in a private school to nurse her mother. She's been living in Hespeler but she has sold her family home and bought a cottage not far from this house. She asked after you. She never married, you know."

Father got up suddenly at that point and excused himself, even though he had not finished his Brown Betty pudding, and went to his study to catch up on his reading.

"Who is Dulcie Trimmer?" Jemma asked.

Aunt got up and went to the kitchen for something.

"She's an old friend of David's," Grandmother

said. "He used to squire her to parties before he met Rose."

"Ruth, you mean," Jemma corrected her.

"Well, he met them both, didn't he?" Grandmother said with the strangest little smirk. I don't know what it meant but it meant something nasty, I could tell. She went on, "We did think he was interested in Rose, at first, but you are quite correct, Jemima. I should have said Ruth."

There was something puzzling in the way she spoke. We all stared at her, all but Theo. Grandmother stared back as if she were daring us to say something. Then she folded up her table napkin and excused herself to go and read the paper.

There we sat deserted by all three grown-ups. That never happens, not at supper. It was odd. Aunt came back though and made sure Theo ate every bite of his dessert.

What they said sounds ordinary written down but it didn't sound one bit ordinary when they said it. That is why I stored it away to write to you. I wonder what this Dulcie is like and why we've never heard of her before.

Tuesday, August 20, 1918

I totally forgot to say before that Jo has been accepted by the University of Toronto Medical

School. She is excited on top and scared to death underneath.

I am glad it isn't like being a probationer nurse. They have to live in a residence and work in the hospital all hours, emptying bedpans and cleaning up vomit and other horrible things. Jo can go to her classes from home, which is lovely.

Wednesday, August 21, 1918

I know I should have written more yesterday but I just could not. I kept thinking about those men in the hospital and their families and how they got hurt and all the ones who will never come home. I couldn't stop crying until Aunt sent Fanny and me out for a tandem ride and gave us some money to buy ice cream. When I came in, I still could not bear to write. I just wanted to get away. So I reread the parts about Beth in *Little Women*. Doing that, I could cry all I wanted without being asked why.

Myrtle, who hardly ever speaks to anyone but Aunt, asked if I had a pain. I told her no and turned my back to the door. She did not stick around.

I feel better today, myself again. I have already promised to go back to the hospital even though Father said it was maybe too much for children of twelve. I don't know why a child of twelve should not face sadness and know the truth of things. We are human beings just like Father and Aunt. When we are there with those men, I don't feel like a "child of twelve." I don't feel like a grown woman quite but I'm on my way.

Thursday, August 22, 1918

I've just been out AGAIN with my funny little brother to feed one of his horses. You did not know that your Uncle Theodore was a horse owner? Well, Jane, according to Theo, the milkman's horse Fred is his friend and looks to him for nourishment. The breadman's horse Betsy is his special chum and has bones sticking out — although she looks perfectly plump to me. There is also the iceman's horse Gertie and the tinker's horse Jasper. There's another I know which I can't remember.

Theo takes them all bread or apples or slices of carrot or even a lick of salt on his little hand and he has to have one of us with him ever since Grandmother told us she had heard, at her Women's Missionary Society meeting, about a child being trodden on by a horse and having her toes crushed. Father said it was nonsense but Aunt cannot risk her darling's little piggies. So somebody has to accompany Theo on his daily errands of mercy.

It is fun really, Jane. I admit to you, but to nobody else, that I like going along. The horses are such great, gentle creatures and they watch for Theo to appear.

Father says that someday a horse will mistake Theo's yellow mop for a haystack and he will come home bald. Father got glared at by everyone but Grandmother and Hamlet. Hamlet did look doleful, but that is the way his face is made. Jowly and owlly.

I go out with Theo when he rides his velocipede too. Aunt is afraid he will get going too fast, ride into the street and get run over. But that tricycle of his, even though it is a Canuck Velocipede, does not go at any great rate when Theo is pedalling. I often put one foot on the bar between the back wheels, and my hands over his, and push off with my other foot. We positively fly and he loves it. Neither of us mentions this to his doting auntie.

Friday, August 23, 1918

We are going to sing to the soldiers again. I don't think I will write about it this time. It hurts me too much. I will tell you if Red Beard does anything comical.

We have been getting Jo outfitted for university. She has told me privately that she plans to have her hair cut before classes begin. For once, she and Jemma will not be in agreement. Jemma can sit on her hair and she is immensely proud of it. I wonder if Jo

will go through with this like Jo in *Little Women*.
Our Josephine has such lovely hair although she
does not think so.

Carrie Galt still wears hers down her back with a
big flat bow at the nape of her neck. She looks jim-
dandy. Jemma keeps quoting the Bible about long
hair being a woman's crowning glory. The strange
part is that Jo's hair is more glorious than Jemma's.
Nobody mentions this to either of them for fear they
will make Jo mad or hurt Jemma's feelings. Jo's is
the exact colour of a polished conker. But Jemma's
is just a deep brown with no red in it. Nice but ordinary.

"Rubbish!" Josephine Macgregor would say to
that.

Aunt wears hers in a roll on the back of her neck
or a bun on the very top when she is dressed up. It
looks elegant when it is in that topknot.

Saturday, August 24, 1918

Jo did get her hair cut. It comes to her shoulders
now. It is still plenty long enough to twist up in a
knob at the back of her neck. She can always put a
rat in it if she wants it to look really long. A rat, Jane,
is a wire coil you wind the hair around to make it
appear longer.

She came home and faced the family, looking like

somebody else. Nobody spoke for a few seconds. Nobody even squeaked. Then Theo went goggle-eyed and asked her where the rest of her hair was and she handed him a bag filled with it. They had gathered it up off the floor. Aunt gave one shriek, blinked back tears and told her she looked "really lovely." But her heart was not in it.

Personally, Jane, I think it is stunning. I didn't know the ends would curl up like that. And when she moves fast, it swings and gleams as it catches the light. I won't say a word now, but when I am older, I will get mine cut the same way.

Grandmother said she had palpitations, of course. Jemma was so quiet and she kept looking at Jo and then, quickly, looking away, as though it hurt her to see her sister changed. They have always worn their hair in the same way before.

Then Father got up and gave her a big hug and Jo cried. Jemma hugged her too but she still looked queer.

Lights Out!

Sunday, August 25, 1918

We went back to the hospital and something astonishing happened. I did not tell even Fan but maybe I should. I stood by that same soldier, the one who has never said a word and does not seem to see.

I began to think about how terribly alone he must feel and I could not help it. When we were singing loudly and nobody was looking, I just reached out and took hold of his hand. I simply stood there, holding it. It was lying palm down, Jane, and, just as I was letting go, he turned it over and held onto me. He is very weak and we both let go in the next second. I know I gasped but nobody noticed because they were singing "Onward, Christian Soldiers."

"Is your name Tom, Dick or Harry?" I murmured, just to be saying something.

I did not expect him to answer and he did not then. But just as they were gathering us to sing a last song, I heard a very low, very husky voice whisper, "Michael."

So, when we were going, I hung back and whispered, "Goodbye, Michael."

He did not answer or turn his head or anything and I left with the group. But, Jane, my knees wobbled as though they were made of junket. I can hardly believe what happened and maybe I should tell someone. But how can I? I should never have taken his hand that way. Grandmother would be too shocked to speak. No, not she. She would lecture me for an hour! Aunt might be, too.

He was just like Theo somehow. I will go once more, I have decided, and then I will know what I should do.

Monday, August 26, 1918

I cannot think of anything but that poor soldier. I think I will have to tell Aunt. Yet I don't know quite how to begin. How can I explain why I picked up his hand that way? Brazen — that's the word they would use for my behaviour. They will be sure to think touching him was forward. If I was a "good girl" I would not have dreamed of doing such a bold thing. Oh, Jane, I feel so confused.

Aunt has started us sewing our clothes for school.

Wednesday, August 28, 1918

We are busy getting ready for school. I have grown a lot taller since last autumn and so has Fan. We would get Jo and Jemma's hand-me-downs except we are bigger. Not just taller but with wider shoulders and longer arms. We take after the Macgregor side, Aunt says. I have to get new shirtwaists and we must make new underthings. Thank goodness Myrtle likes hemming! She's good at it, too. Her little stitches are all even and Aunt keeps making me study them. This is when I have caught Myrtle actually smiling.

Aunt bought us some wide lace to trim our petticoats with. It will make them longer. But it is beastly to sew on. Worth it though. It is so pretty, it makes me feel almost rich. And of course I have lots of hat ribbons, thanks to that horse! I have already used some just to tie up the back of my hair with a big bow. It looked splendid.

Our class will be the oldest students this year, going into Entrance. Maybe they will call it something different when you are my age, Jane. It means "high school entrance" and when it is done, we write Entrance exams. The Grade Eight students have always seemed so important. And now I'm about to become one.

Thursday, August 29, 1918

I took a break from *Pride and Prejudice* and got started reading *The Rosary* by Florence Barclay. I couldn't stop. Aunt says it is a silly book but she loves it anyway. Me too. It is so romantic. Of course, I made the blind hero look just like my blind soldier at the hospital. I cried buckets. And I skipped and skimmed enough to finish it before Aunt told us to put out the light.

But the people in *The Rosary* are not real like Elizabeth and Jane Bennet. Having Mrs. B. for a mother would be a terrible trial. It would be better to be motherless like Fan and me, I think. She would embarrass us every time we had to go out with her.

Sunday, September 1, 1918

The War news is still terrible. I can't write about that.

I have a new pleated skirt that swings out almost straight when I whirl around. Fan has one too but, for once, Aunt let us choose different colours. Mine is a deep blue and Fan's is chocolate brown.

I am going to wear mine next time we go to the hospital — if Aunt does not forbid me. I promise not to twirl.

Father just came in and told us that our troops have broken through the Hindenburg Line! That is really important. Father says that it was the German line of defence and they believed it could not be broken.

"The casualties must be staggering," Aunt said in a low voice.

"But the end is coming, Rose," Father said and he put his hand on her shoulder. It was strange. Until I saw her reach up to touch his hand, I did not realize that I have never seen him touch her before, not that I can remember anyway. I think touching Michael's hand made me notice. I don't know why but it seemed special.

She was right about the casualties. "Thousands," the paper said.

Myrtle was sick today so we had to do the washing without her. It was my job to hang out the clothes. I got so entranced by the sunshine and the wind in the trees and the exciting feeling of school starting up soon, that I allowed myself to sit down on the grass for "a minute." Then I sort of stretched out and gave my eyes a rest by letting the lids slip closed. Theo came running to wake me. He got me hanging up the towels seconds before Aunt came out with fire in her eye. She stared at me, took in what little was hanging on the line and Theo's presence. He was blushing and staring at his boots. He can't bear to make his darling Mama mad at him. She stood there steaming for a moment. Then she did an about-turn.

"Well done, Theo," she tossed back over her shoulder. "Keep her at it."

Then she marched back into the house like a sergeant major.

Well done indeed.

How do you think I'll do as a writer, Jane? I was trying to make the scene come to life because otherwise this was an extremely dull day.

I thought the Hindenburg Line had been broken but it is still in the news. I can't imagine it.

I also have trouble imagining school beginning

tomorrow in spite of all our sewing. But starting a new year is always an adventure — or that is how it feels to me.

Tuesday, September 3, 1918

School! We are still Jesse Ketchum students even though we have been turned out of our own building by the army once again. We are so crowded. Now we are bigger, Mr. Briggs says we must maintain our separate identity. We are supposed to have a desk each but there isn't enough room.

Mr. Briggs is the principal and the teacher of Grade Eight, both of them. Homework already.

I'll write again tomorrow, Jane. Aunt is calling me to come and fold sheets. We do it when Myrtle is not here because, when she helps, she drops her corner if you jerk it the least bit. And we have a lot of sheets to fold.

Wednesday, September 4, 1918

I really do like Mr. Briggs. The others say he is too strict but he has a twinkle in his eye. He does not give even the boys the strap all the time like Mr. Short did last year. I hate it when they give anyone the strap. You can hear it strike their hand and you can hear them whimper after the first few licks. It is horrible. I am grateful that hardly anybody gives girls the strap. Some teachers do, I have heard, but none has ever done it to a girl in my class.

This is an old school but not as old as Jesse Ketchum. I like knowing that lots of other boys and girls have walked the halls before I was born, leaving hollowed out places on the steps. Fan says a new school would be better. It wouldn't smell of old chalk dust. I think all schools, old or new, smell of Arithmetic. "What does that smell like?" she wanted to know. "Dry," I told her and she laughed. I love making my sister laugh. She's so given to just smiling that Mona Lisa smile.

Thursday, September 5, 1918

The War news sounds better but still very unsettled.

Pixie had a fit today. I thought she was dying. She went stiff and her eyes rolled up and her legs jerked. But she came out of it.

Aunt cried and held her in her arms. I cried too but it was seeing Aunt's tears that started mine. After all, Pixie is practically an antique. Aunt has had her since she was younger than Hamlet.

Friday, September 6, 1918

Another part of the Hindenburg Line has been "breached" — some key section, Father says. But thousands of lives were lost. It is supposed to be tremendously important, but I think of all the mothers and sisters hearing the news.

That is enough of that. I can't keep dwelling on it or I will get the page all wet and the ink will run. I make enough inkblots without that.

Saturday, September 7, 1918

I don't know what came over Aunt but we had to help with housecleaning all day. Beat rugs, washed curtains, polished furniture and the banisters, even washed the windows with vinegar and brown paper. Like Jack's crown in the nursery rhyme book. I am getting mixed up. Too bad Myrtle does not come on weekends. I am too worn out to write sensibly. Poor Jane.

Later

I finally saw the mysterious Dulcie Trimmer and it was spooky! As a break from the "eternal round of housework," Aunt sent me to the bakery to get Theo a gingerbread boy because he is sick and feeling sorry for himself. There are tea tables at the front and there sat Grandmother with somebody I'd never seen before. When she saw me, she called me over and introduced me to Miss Trimmer.

"This is my granddaughter Fiona," she said. "You

remember I told you about David's two sets of twins?"

Miss Trimmer nodded and smiled. She kept on smiling and smiling in the oddest way. You could not help noticing because she has such large teeth and they are so white. They would make a great advertisement for Pepsodent toothpaste. I could not think what made her smile seem strange for a couple of minutes and then I figured it out. It never changed. It didn't get broader or turn up at one corner more than the other. It was fixed — like the smile on a doll. But her eyes moved up and down, taking in every inch of me in the rudest way, as though I was a specimen of some kind. She made me feel I had grease spots on my shirtwaist or a smudge on my nose.

"I knew your father very well indeed before he went off to that foolish war," she said with a strange little chuckle to end off her words. "David and I were SUCH dear friends, weren't we, Mrs. Macgregor?"

When she said "such" she cooed it, pulling it out long like taffy. Jane, she actually simpered at Grandmother, and Grandmother simpered right back and gave a little nod to clinch it, whatever it was.

"That's nice," I said and ran. I was out on the sidewalk before I remembered I had forgotten to buy Theo's gingerbread.

Luckily there is another bakery not far up the street so I ran to Guthries and got him one of theirs. He didn't notice but Aunt did. She asked why I went to the shop that was further away.

"Grandmother and Dulcie Trimmer were having tea in the first one," I told her.

"Oh," she said, as though she understood perfectly. Then she added, "Miss Trimmer to you, young lady."

"Miss Trimmer," I said meekly, hoping I could get her to talk. "Aunt, was that Dulcie Trimmer really a great friend of Father's in the olden days?"

"I told you to call her Miss Trimmer," Aunt snapped. Then she grinned at me and muttered, "That creature gives me the pip. Your grandmother has invited her here for tea tomorrow. Ruth told me once that your grandmother thought she was a great catch and hoped David would propose to her."

I sat down and tried to pry more out of her. But she gave me a little push and laughed and said, "Enough of that, Fiona Rose. You run along and entertain your little brother. He's beside himself because I'm keeping him in the house until his sore throat is completely better."

So I had no chance to find out anything more about the mystery woman, Jane. You should have seen the look that went back and forth between Grandmother and D. Trimmer when she told her I was "one of David's two sets of twins." She gives me the pip, too.

I have just had a revelation! I am almost positive Dulcie T.'s coming to tea is what got Aunt started on her housecleaning frenzy. Aha! The Macgregor family must put its best foot — or feet — forward.

Sunday, September 8, 1918

We went to the hospital again and the strangest thing happened. Michael was not there. I could not believe it. At last, I asked the nurse who was passing and she said, "Oh, it was a miracle. Just after you were here last time, he spoke to one of the nurses, Miss Reynolds. He remembered his name."

She was turning away but I grabbed her sleeve. "What was it?" I asked her.

She gave me a funny look. So did the girls standing near. Tillie Osborne snickered. She's vulgar. Nancy Spry muttered, "Watch it, Matilda."

But then the nurse told me. "Michael Franks," she said.

Then she, too, sent Tillie a glare that settled her hash. "He's been moved to a recuperation ward where they can work with him toward his recovery. When he spoke, we couldn't believe it. It was SUCH a shock!"

"Fiona, are you joining us?" Miss Banks said, so I

had to go. I almost burst out crying but only a little bit of it was because I missed him. I am so happy he is getting well. And I told Fan finally. She was fascinated but said not to tell Aunt. So I won't. I wonder if I helped him even the tiniest bit. At least, I know now that I did him no harm.

I wish Aunt would play Beethoven's "Song of Joy." But when we got home, Dulcie Trimmer had just left and Aunt was on her way up to her room for a rest. She looked tired out so I think I will start the supper as a surprise.

Monday, September 9, 1918

I have memory work to learn. It is by Alfred Lord Tennyson. I like it but it is sad. It begins,

Sunset and evening star,
And one clear call for me!
And may there be no moaning of the bar,
When I put out to sea,
But such a tide as moving seems asleep,
Too full for sound and foam,
When that which drew from out the boundless
    deep
Turns again home.

I like the beginning bit best. The same with the second verse.

Twilight and evening bell,
And after that the dark!
And may there be no sadness of farewell,
When I embark . . .

It is about dying. I hope nobody close to me dies until we are very, very old. I guess it can't be helped then. Maybe you don't even mind. Fan has to learn a poem about dying too but it is shorter. It is by Robert Louis Stevenson and it starts out,

Under the wide and starry sky,
Dig the grave and let me lie.
Glad did I live and gladly die,
And I laid me down with a will.

It is more cheerful than mine but not so poetic. Father has told me about him. He was sick a lot and went to live in the South Seas. I wonder if he really died gladly. It is hard to believe anyone could.
Every night, Theo prays,

Now I lay me down to sleep,
I pray the Lord my soul to keep.
If I should die before I wake,
I pray the Lord my soul to take.

I don't think he hears what he is praying. I hope not.

Tuesday, September 10, 1918

Mr. Briggs made us write a pretend page in a diary this morning. He read mine out to the whole class.

"Teacher's pet, as usual," Annie Cray whispered. I smiled my sweetest smile at her. She had just been taken over by the green-eyed monster. I had an unfair advantage, after all. Most of them have had no practice in diary writing. I told about the horse stepping on my hat ribbon. Everybody laughed. Annie described the weather. She sits right in front of me so I read every boring word.

Poor old Annie.

Wednesday, September 11, 1918

Oh, Jane, I have my pen in my hand but I am too tired to write with it. Mathematics homework. Ugh!

Thursday, September 12, 1918

Jane, life seems so crowded with busyness. Soon I will sit down and catch up the bits I am missing. Mr. Briggs made us write a composition on Patriotism. It was hard. Father says it has nothing to do with bugles blowing and flags flying but is all about loving your land enough to face trench warfare to save it. I don't like topics like "Duty" or "Patriotism" or "Courage." I'd so much rather write a story or a poem.

We were supposed to sing to the soldiers again tomorrow but Miss Banks is so busy with her schoolwork that we had to put it off.

I'm too sleepy to keep writing tonight, Jane. Sleep well.

Friday, September 13, 1918

It is Friday the thirteenth. Everybody talked about it at breakfast. Grandmother, who had come down early, said there was truth in most old superstitions. She believed in being very careful not to do anything rash on Friday the thirteenth.

Then, when we came home, we found that Aunt had had a letter from a school friend of hers who lives in Quebec. The terrible thing is that her son came safely home from War, sent home for some reason I forget, and then got sick with what they call the Spanish Flu. (I don't really understand why it is called the Spanish Flu.) His sister caught it from him. He died after only four days but his sister pulled through after being "at death's door" for nearly two weeks. Their mother wrote that others seem to be stricken down with this disease and it is surprising because they were young and strong.

Grandmother says she must be exaggerating and Father said it was hard to believe. Aunt told them that they clearly did not know her friend, who was very down-to-earth and never exaggerated anything. Then she went upstairs and did not come back down for over an hour.

"Thank fortune we don't have such diseases in this province," Grandmother muttered.

"You don't get Influenza from speaking French," Jo snorted. Then she left the table too.

Quebec does seem a bit unreal to me and very far away. But I am sorry for that family.

Saturday, September 14, 1918

Aunt decided today would be a perfect time to turn all the mattresses and she made Fanny and me help. Before we knew it, we were doing an extra wash of bedding and beating the dust out of the small rugs and shaking up the pillows. It's a wonder she didn't send us out to some farm to get fresh feathers to stuff the pillows. I do not think adults should have the right to take children's one weekly holiday away and use it up on humdrum chores. It was funny though to find out what was hidden under Jemma's mattress. I will not write it in here since I didn't actually read any of the letters tied up with a blue ribbon — but I might have if Aunt had not watched me like a hawk. Who on earth would write such treasured letters to our Jemima?

We played croquet after supper. This time, Jemma

accused Jo of cheating. "As usual," she said. But she was laughing when she said it. It was loads of fun.

Sunday, September 15, 1918

The minister prayed for our army again. He asked God to strike down our enemies and lead our gallant troops to victory. I think it is fine but Father always gets restless as though something about it bothers him. I was going to ask him about this but he seems a bit like a stranger when we come home from church and he shuts himself up in his study.

I thought about going after him but I asked Aunt instead. She says he reads the names of those who have fallen and he thinks of all the other fathers in England and even in Germany reading the same sort of lists.

"We humans made this War, not God," she told me. "David thinks it is up to us to work it out and we should not be expecting God to strike down our enemies when most of them are young men just like ours."

"Is Father a pacifist?" I asked her.

"He would have enlisted if he had been physically fit," she said. "They would not take a man his age with a limp and five children. But he certainly believes there are better ways to settle problems than going to war and killing people."

Then she blew her nose and went off into her bedroom.

It is all hard to understand, Jane, and I do wish the War would get done with, the way Father keeps saying it will. Then I could stop worrying over it, couldn't I? Maybe. I think there must be things to do after a war to set things straight.

Watching Theo do a follow-the-dots puzzle in the paper, with the tip of his tongue sticking out, comforted me. He looked so solemn.

Monday, September 16, 1918

The porridge was burnt this morning just like the porridge in *Jane Eyre*. But Aunt threw it all out and made us boiled eggs and toast with jam.

I think I will start reading a new book. I finished *Pride and Prejudice*. Aunt asked me if I wanted another one by Jane Austen but I told her not yet and started *The Harvester* over again. I like the heroine's name being Ruth.

Tuesday, September 17, 1918

This was too tedious a day to bother recording. We are having our first tests at the end of the week and I need to study. I hate it. I also have to work on the nightgown I am sewing for my Household Sciences class. I loathe sewing. I am forever pricking my finger and Myrtle is not there to do the hemming for me. Miss Dalrimple won't let us take it home and do it on our treadle sewing machine. We have to learn to make different stitches by hand and how to darn and hem. As if most of us have not been taught those dreary skills at home!

Aunt suggested that I should tell Miss Dalrimple that I wear pyjamas, but I am afraid that if I did, she would say I had to sew a pair of those. It would be two garments, even worse than the nightgown.

Thursday, September 19, 1918

The music teacher came today and taught us "Do you ken John Peel?" It was fun to sing! But it is not very Canadian. I've never seen anyone ride out hunting foxes that way. Then we sang, "Flow Gently, Sweet Afton," which is at least romantic, followed by "The Skye Boat Song." The music teacher is British, Jane.

At breakfast Father told us that he had read, in *The Toronto Daily Star,* that they had cases of Influenza in the military hospitals, but they were under quarantine and the authorities saw no need for concern.

"I hope they know what they are talking about," he said.

Both he and Aunt shot glances at my little brother, who has the sniffles again. It is as though that child is the only person in this house of any real importance. I am fond of Theo myself but they are besotted with him!

I coughed. Nobody noticed.

Friday, September 20, 1918

Jo and Carrie are attending classes but it is not easy. The girls in the class meet outside the lecture room and walk in together. Carrie has a cousin her mother's age who was one of the very first women doctors to qualify. When she and her friends marched in, the male students would stamp their feet and chant,

She doesn't know that her degree
Should be M-R-S and not M-D.

I do not want to be a doctor. I think, if I have a career, I want to write books. But such mean taunts are almost enough to make you sign up for Meds just so you could stick out your tongue at those stupid boys or hold your head high at least while you stalked past.

Jo says it is important that the girls act very grown-up and prove that they have brains and are not going just to try to catch a male medical student as a husband, the way Grandmother said the other night at supper. Even Father, who usually pretends not to hear her, turned and glared at her. "That comment is unworthy of you, Mother," he said in a voice like ice.

Grandmother blushed. It was a dull, patchy blush but still, I truly believe she was ashamed of herself. Good for Father!

They have one professor who turns his back when the girls come into the lecture hall and who does not speak to them. He never looks at them properly either. Everybody knows he does not believe women should be doctors. I cannot understand it. Half the people in the world are female. He thinks it is a waste to train them when they will just end up getting married and never practising. Grandmother says he has a point.

Jo claims she will not marry a man who will not let her practise her profession. Grandmother gave one of her snorts but she did not go on to say more, not with Father's eye fixed on her.

Monday, September 23, 1918

The weekend was full to bursting with visitors. Aunt Jessica and Uncle Walter came with their obnoxious children. We couldn't go to sing. I was almost glad. I feel as though the heart has gone out of it. Visitors would be fine if they didn't make so much work. So many dishes to wash! So many dishes to dry! And guess who had to put them all away! I wonder if Theo gets out of everything because he is so small or partly because he is a boy.

Well, at least some women have the vote now. Maybe, by the time I am as old as Aunt, all women will.

Thursday, September 26, 1918

Jane, have you given me up for lost? It is just that there is a lot more homework to do in Grade Eight. Mathematics is my bugbear.

But I will have time and energy soon, I promise. Not tonight though. I still have to draw a map of Canada with all nine provinces and put in the capital cities. I was moaning to Aunt about it.

"Thank the good Lord that you aren't a Yankee with forty-eight states to draw," she said.

Trust Aunt.

Friday, September 27, 1918

Got the darn map finished and knocked the ink bottle over so a great stream flowed right across everything east of Ontario. But I think I can trace the uninky provinces now the paper has dried.

Saturday, September 28, 1918

Jane, why did I want to keep this diary? If it weren't for you, I would lose it accidentally on purpose. I am reading a book I cannot bear to leave. It is called *T. Tembarom*. It is like *Little Lord Fauntleroy* for grown-ups. I can't tear myself away one moment longer.

Sunday, September 29, 1918

We went to the hospital today. Oh, Jane, I thought writing to you about it might help but I can't do it. I keep crying. Fan has gone to get Aunt. Maybe I will tell you later.

Later

I think I can tell you about it now, Jane, but quickly, because I have to help with supper. We were at the hospital and I had to go to the bathroom so I asked where it was and set out. I opened the wrong door. It was a ward for men who are shell-shocked or something. They were so pitiful. Oh, I cannot tell you the details. One man was lying there with no legs. Another one was yelling gibberish and then burst into tears like a baby.

Father says I am not to go back. The older ones will go but not Fan and me. Fan told me, privately, that she was glad. I hope Jo is not too ashamed of us.

Michael Frank was not in that room. I was glad of that.

Aunt says she is relieved to have us stop because there just might be somebody with Influenza brought there. Miss Banks said she had been assured it was safe, but she is inclined to agree that we should put off our visiting for a few weeks.

Monday, September 30, 1918

Fall has come. The maples are touched with scarlet and the leaves on our silver birches are growing yellow. One of Jemma's friends said there could not be a God with all the suffering in the world and Jemma told us she just said, "Nobody can look at the maples and not believe in God."

"Good for you, daughter," Father said.

Jemma went pink. He doesn't smile that way often. He laughs at her jokes but this time, his smile said he was proud of her. Usually it is Jo who makes him look that way.

Tuesday, October 1, 1918

I have a headache. Sorry, Jane. It is NOT a Flu symptom, I promise. But I can't write with the letters swimming in front of my eyes the way they are doing. I am afraid to tell Father because he would take me to the doctor and get me spectacles.

"Megrims," Grandmother snorted when Aunt told me to go and lie down. She has no use for people who give in to such minor ailments. It is a good thing I don't know how to strike someone dead or I might have done it.

Wednesday, October 2, 1918

People are becoming anxious about this Influenza even though the Public Health doctor says we should just keep fit and not catch colds. Otherwise, we're not to worry. As if worry could make us sick.

Thursday, October 3, 1918

A little girl died of the Spanish Flu in Toronto General Hospital four days ago. Jo came home and told Aunt. If she is the child Jo thinks she was, we have all seen her. She was in one of the primary classes at Jesse Ketchum and once in a while she came to our Sunday School. I think her name was Jenny or Janie Robertson but I am not certain.

They are considering placing our school under quarantine. I think that means shutting it down. Yet when you are under quarantine for scarlet fever, you are shut up in your house, not shut out of it, so I don't understand exactly what it means. We'll find out tomorrow.

Friday, October 4, 1918

The paper says that the Flu has definitely arrived in Ontario. There are lots of people in Renfrew who have it. And a man of thirty-two has died.

Fanny and I did not even get to go to school. Aunt announced at breakfast that we are staying home, quarantine or no quarantine.

"I will not risk the lives of my children," she announced.

Nobody but me seemed to notice she had called us her children. But she should because we are hers. We all feel that way, even the Almost Twins who knew Mother the longest.

Just imagine, Jane. No school!

"No school does not mean you are to start in on any high jinks," Aunt said then in her sternest voice.

Fanny put on a serious expression but I could not stop grinning. If I could have turned a cartwheel, I would have. I said so and Theo bounced up from the chair where he was sitting and turned two for me.

Poor Hamlet looked deeply disturbed while his boy was upside down, but wagged his tail like mad when Theo turned right side up again.

"That hound is a honey," I said.

Then Theo told me, solemnly, that Great Danes are not hounds. I opened my mouth to ask him what sort of dog they are but did not. I am sure he has no idea and he had just made me a present of two elegant cartwheels. I am working on being a thoughtful big sister.

Aunt says we still must study and, with Father being an English teacher, I know we will have to, whether we want to or not. I do not admit it to anyone, not even Fan, but I like learning most things. I don't even mind writing examinations in the subjects I enjoy: English Composition, English Grammar, English Literature and History. But studying them at home will be much more pleasant. I get fidgets sitting next to Fanny in our double desk. If I wiggle too much, she keeps the teacher from noticing by coughing or laughing or doing something small to distract him. Here at home, I can lie on my stomach on our bed while I read or even climb a tree, as long as I take a schoolbook with me.

Later

Aunt went to the market and came home looking smug. Some of the women were worrying that you could catch Flu from eating unwrapped bread or a loaf handled by a sick person.

"I felt like telling them to buy some yeast and

flour and get busy," Aunt sniffed.

She makes all our bread. When Fanny and I come home and open the door and the smell gushes out, our friends who were about to walk away come back with their tongues hanging out, hoping for a slice.

Father says that the word "lady" really means someone who kneads bread. If you don't make bread, you are not a lady! I think many women would not believe this notion of Father's, but he showed me the word root in his big dictionary. We are both interested in where words come from.

Bedtime

The Flu is becoming big news even though almost nobody here has come down with it. Grandmother was reading *The Star* and announced that she was disgusted with the stuff they put in the newspaper. What got her goat was an undertaker saying he had had fifteen funerals to do. I still don't know whether they were all in one week or what.

Father said they were thinking of closing the high school too. He is worried about his students. I'll bet they are not worried. They will be as pleased as I am.

It will be strange having my father at home when he's usually at school.

In Ottawa, everything is shutting down, Father tells us. Theatres, churches, schools, pool halls, bowling alleys. He read this from a letter he got.

"Well, the disease has accomplished one great benefit then," Grandmother said.

Do you know what she meant, Jane? Shutting down pool rooms. She calls them "dens of iniquity."

"But, Mother," Father said sweetly, "I thought you believed in attending church."

When I write it, it doesn't sound so funny, but it was. I thought Grandmother would choke.

Sunday, October 6, 1918

We sang three of my favourite hymns at church. "And Did Those Feet in Ancient Times" and "Will Your Anchor Hold" and "Lead, Kindly Light." Father says I have eclectic tastes. I'll have to look that one up. Maybe it just means I like lots of different kinds of hymns. That is true.

I hope you like to sing, Jane. I love singing while I do dishes or make beds. It makes work go faster. Father says that is why there are sea shanties.

Monday, October 7, 1918

I'm in my room after having a flaming row with Grandmother. Here is exactly what happened, Jane. I can take my time telling you since she told me to stay here until I was ready to apologize for my insolence. I may have to spend the rest of my life in this bedroom, since I am NOT sorry.

It blew up after I brought Ruby Whiting in with me to escape from some boys who were calling her names. When she went home after eating a piece of Aunt's bread, Grandmother said I should know better than to associate with the Whitings. "They are common as dirt. David brought that girl's father home once and we told him not to bring him again. He said the boy was fine but we knew better and we were right. Look where he is now!"

I did not know where Ruby's father was. She never talks about him. But the boys yelled, "Your old man's in the clink." I think that means prison. I told Grandmother that I didn't know anything about her father, but Ruby is a nice girl and my friend. Then I said I'd have her over whenever I liked. Grandmother pointed her finger at the stairs and gave me my marching orders. I longed to yell, "I don't have to do what you say. You're not my mother!" But I managed not to.

After a talk with Father

Father came up to see what had happened. I told him. "Just because she says things like 'My auntie come over last night' and 'Youse have a real nice house' doesn't mean she's common, does it?" I asked him. "If Ruby is common, she is much kinder and far more polite than Grandmother."

Father corrects us when we make mistakes in grammar, but Ruby doesn't have anyone to tell her how to speak properly. I don't think she'll ever come back to our house, not after the way Grandmother stared right through her and said to her, "I think you'd best be running along," in her coldest voice.

Father rubbed his chin, the way he does when he's thinking. Then he said Mr. Whiting is in jail for getting drunk and neglecting his family. He said he is proud of me for standing up for Ruby. Then he got stuck.

I finally said I would come down and apologize if he really wanted me to and he said, "It's a steep price to pay for peace but I would appreciate it, Fiona." And just before he left, he said I should play with Ruby at school but perhaps not bring her here since she would be made to feel uncomfortable. Then he went out and, just as I picked up my diary, Jane, he stuck his head back in and said he counted on me to continue to treat the English language with respect, taking him as my model.

Now he has run down the stairs whistling "The Maple Leaf Forever," leaving me to make up my mind to lie to my grandmother and say I am sorry when I am not in the least.

I am really sorry for Ruby though. Her family sounds something like Pearl's in Mrs. McClung's book *Sowing Seeds in Danny*. It is terrible what people do when they get drunk. We had to sign The Pledge at Mission Band saying we promised never to drink alcohol. When I told Father, he just said, "Never is a long time, daughter." But I think he is a teetotaller. I've never seen anybody drink alcohol. I don't think we have any in the house.

Tuesday, October 8, 1918

In *The Star* yesterday, it said there are lots more people with the Flu. Fifty-three more cases, I think. A few have even died! One was a girl only a year younger than Jo and Jemma and she was only sick a short time before she died. It still seems unreal to me but I am trying to think how it must be for her family. She died at home. It didn't say if the rest of them caught it.

I hate Mathematics. Simple arithmetic is all right but now we are doing problems with percents and interest and using decimals all the time. I can't get it right. Aunt tries to help me but I think she hates it too. Jo thinks we are crazy. She actually said Algebra is beautiful! Aunt snorted at that. Fan does the problems without trouble. Yet I am a much better speller than she is! It is puzzling when we come from the same home and have always had the same teachers.

Friday, October 11, 1918

Can't write tonight, Jane. I feel sick and I have what Aunt calls "a pain under my pinny." I wonder if you know what she means.

Saturday morning, October 12, 1918

Somebody threw something poisonous over our fence and Hamlet ate whatever it was before we could stop him. He is still alive but, Jane, when a Great Dane brings up his boots, it is positively disgusting. Theo showered the dog with sympathy and helped clean up the mess he made on the hall carpet. Theo is a noble boy.

I guess Hamlet saved Pixie's life because when she went to see what he was eating, he growled at her, which he never does. I know he couldn't have known, but it is something to think about.

Flu stories are coming in thick and fast. Aunt is now worried about Jo going into the hospital but Jo says she is just sitting in lectures so far and Aunt can relax. They have not seen one live patient. "Nor a dead one, come to that," she tacked on.

I hope she's not stringing Aunt a line to keep her happy.

Grandmother told us that her friend Dulcie Trimmer says half the nurses in Grace Hospital are down with this "scourge."

Jo laughed. "I'm not a nurse nor am I at Grace Hospital," she said, "but I'll be careful not to do anything foolish."

Then she told them they should maybe send me and Fanny out of the city for a bit. And, before we could get in on the discussion, we were ordered up to bed. It is no good trying to listen, either. Father sits where he can see all the way to the head of the stairs.

Sunday, October 13, 1918

Today is Thanksgiving Sunday. Usually we would be in church singing thankful hymns, but we did not go because of the Flu. Then, after we had finished eating our turkey dinner, Father told us that after we were sent upstairs last night, the doctor came around and said that he is sure now that Hamlet's master, who died so unexpectedly, had Spanish Flu. Dr. Musgrave did not realize it at the time. He thought it was just bronchitis and did not connect it up with his patient's having been in Quebec. But he was the executor for the man's will, and, when he tried to get in touch with his relations in Montreal, they had had the Spanish Flu. Some had died. As Father told us this, even I could see how upset he was. But I did not dream, Jane, that because people we had never even met had had this Flu, Fanny and I would be sent out of the city for a while. I am to go to Grandma and Grandy's near Mimico and Fanny is going to stay with Uncle Walter and Aunt Jessica near Sunnyside.

Jo and Jemma have declared that they cannot leave Toronto. Jemma is at Normal School and Jo is some weeks into her classes at U of T. Jo admits they are talking of putting a quarantine on the university students. Aunt is not letting Theo out of the house except in the back garden with Hamlet. The back garden has a high fence around it. And she goes out with him to make sure he doesn't start calling out to the neighbours. He would do just that. He's the friendliest boy alive. Hamlet would keep them from going through the gate, though. He is so enormous that nobody dares get chummy with him.

Fanny can't come to Grandma and Grandy's with me because they have Tim and Pansy with them for the summer. They are children of a friend of hers who had infantile paralysis last summer and can't look after the children when they are not in school. Grandma is forever helping her out. The woman can only use one hand and she has a brace on her leg.

I was so flabbergasted when they told us we were all leaving that I just sat there with my mouth hanging open. Fanny, however, surprised everyone by bursting into tears. She howled that we could not be separated. Father was very stern and said that we could not ask our family members to take two of us. Then he said that we were not the only children being sent out of Toronto until the Flu outbreak is over.

It makes me feel strange, I do confess, but I am not upset the way Fanny is. She is usually so easy-going and there she sat with tears running down her cheeks. Everyone stared at her. I think I may even be excited. I have never been away from her in my whole life and it will be interesting to see how I get along on my own. I feel it may be an adventure. It should not be for long, after all.

I won't tell Fan this, however. She is still blotchy with tears and looks as woebegone as Hamlet. He feels for her and keeps licking her cheeks. She should be grateful.

Monday, October 14, 1918
At Grandma's

They did not waste any time getting us on our way. We no sooner heard we were going than Aunt started us packing. I was deposited here well before bedtime last night. Dr. Musgrave drove me in his car. Uncle Walter and Aunt Jessica were to come later to fetch Fanny. We really should have a car of our own, but Father says walking is good for us.

As usual, Grandma hugged me and kept saying

how wonderful it was to have me with them for a proper visit and Grandy just gave a quick salute and a wink and went back to his book. But I knew he was as glad to see me as she was. He just doesn't say more than he needs to.

It was queer waking up in a strange room in a bed without Fan in it. At home, one of our bedroom windows faces east and, except in midwinter, we are wakened by the rising sun. Here my room faces north and no sun ever creeps in. I don't think I have ever slept in a bed by myself before.

Pansy has a small cot to herself. She is a nice little girl but she is only nine and given to giggling. She also wraps herself around me and clings. Tim is twelve, like me, but has no use for girls. He's found a family of boys down the road and he spends most of his time with them.

Grandy was always quiet but now he hardly speaks at all. Grandma told me, when he was out of earshot, that he doesn't know what to do with himself now that the work of the farm is done by others.

"Don't mind him, Fiona dear," she murmured. "He loves you as much as ever. He worries about the War news too. I am grateful that he enjoys reading and that we have lots of books to keep him content."

Nobody around here has had the Flu yet and it is almost as though they do not quite believe in it, although Grandy looks very serious and shakes his head whenever it is mentioned.

What a strange Thanksgiving! I wonder how Fan is.

Tuesday night, October 15, 1918

Two and a half days without Fanny. It does seem unreal. I am so used to sharing things with her.

We don't have to go to school while we are here but Grandma used to teach in a one-room schoolhouse down the road and she has us busy learning spelling words and poetry. She is making me read aloud to her this enormous poem called "Gray's Elegy in a Country Churchyard." It is sad but very peaceful. Grandma had a friend who went to England once and visited the very graveyard where the man sat under a tree to write it. She said the tree was still there. Well, trees can live a long time. There is a beech tree near our house that is over one hundred years old. It was there when Toronto was called Muddy York. Maybe. I am never certain about dates. But I do know that beech tree has seen the world change around it as it grew. It rustled its leaves and told me so.

Theo and I both believe trees talk to us. We don't tell other people because we know they will not understand. Not even Fanny has heard them.

Nobody talks about the War here. I am not sure why.

Wednesday, October 16, 1918

I actually found part of a newspaper Grandma had put out in the trash. I didn't say anything but I took it up to my room and read it. I'll copy in some of it, Jane, so you can see what is so worrying us these days.

New civilian cases reported today hover around 300 in the hospitals, another 170 at homes. More than 40 deaths in the previous 24 hours. "There are people in the city who are almost hysterical for fear they will contract the disease," says Dr. Hastings. "For goodness' sake, let everyone keep cool."

His own daughter is recovering after falling ill the previous day. A baker put an ad in *The Star* notifying customers half his delivery staff is down with the Flu.

It does sound bad and also muddled. There was a sheet from October 11th too, filled with War news. Canada is beset at home and overseas both. Here is a bit of it, Jane.

OCTOBER 11

The Canadians, exhausted after days of unremitting fighting, finally drove the Germans out of their most important remaining distribution centre, Cambrai.

Without Father to explain what I read, I don't truly understand it. He shows us where things are on a map of Europe. But Grandy does not seem to say much about what is going on in the world and

Grandma has no maps that I have seen, and asking her would only upset her.

I feel far away from home these days.

Thursday, October 17, 1918

I got a letter from Fan today! It was so amazing to see her writing. It came in an envelope for Grandma, from Aunt. She is missing me. I had not missed her so very much until the letter came. Ever since I read it, I have felt like crying my eyes out.

Fanny left after I did. Before Uncle Walter came for her, she tells me, Father read from the paper that in Manitoba you could be sent to jail for spitting on the street. Theo asked where Manitoba was and, when he was sure it was far away, he said he was going out to spit in the garden while it was still safe.

That bit made me laugh through my tears. It made Grandy laugh right out loud too, which was lovely. He is so quiet mostly, as though he is in some faraway place.

The No Spitting law is to guard against spreading the Flu, of course. It took Aunt quite a lecture to persuade Theo that spitting was not allowed. EVER!

He is definitely a dear boy, Jane. I missed him terribly when I read that story.

Today Grandma packed a big picnic basket and hitched up Florence to the old pony trap and took the three of us for a jaunt up the river. We were gone all day. We even put our toes in the water, although we pulled them right back out. The water was cold as ice. Grandma can skip stones better than anybody. Tim is good, but not a patch on her. After we had finished eating, we sat in the sunshine and she read us the story of Rikki-tikki-tavi. Jane, if I have never read it to you, tell me to get the book and we will read it at once. Rikki-tikki is the smartest little mongoose. I wish there was one in our garden but we have no cobras. Rikki would not like to live where he could not kill cobras.

By the time we got home, we were shivering even wrapped in the steamer rugs Grandma brought along. Aunt would certainly have disapproved of us getting chilled. All the doctors tell you not to worry about the Influenza and then tell you to take great care to remain healthy.

I do hope poor Theo is not being forced to swallow extra cod liver oil.

That will be the last picnic of 1918. Maybe, by summertime 1919, the War and the Flu will both have ended.

Friday, October 18, 1918

Grandma told us this morning that many, many women are signing up to become "Sisters of Service." They attend three lectures to know what to do, and get a blue-and-white satin S.O.S. badge, before heading out to back up the public health nurses and all the rest of the helpers, who must be wearing out.

Another letter from Fanny, Jane. They have stopped people borrowing books from the library! That is terrible. It is a good thing I am not home because I go to the library every week.

Our church is running a soup kitchen to help out. I feel very far away.

Fanny ends up by saying, oh so lightly, that Jemma is volunteering to be a Sister of Service. I thought she might.

How is Fanny keeping so well informed out at Aunt Jessica's? I cannot understand, although I am glad of any news.

Saturday, October 19, 1918

I think Grandma is worried about our being homesick so she plans expeditions or gives us jobs to do. We washed the windows yesterday. Grandma climbed out on the windowsill and did the outside panes. I was scared she would fall but she was steady as the North Star. Grandy laughed at me when I said I was afraid she would fall.

"She hasn't fallen since she fell in love with me,"

he said, his eyes twinkling at her.

She teaches us to do things, too. She has actually got me embroidering the end of a pillowcase for Aunt for Christmas. It has pretty flowers and tiny leaves and three beautiful drops of my lifeblood on it.

How do you think my family is, Jane? I have an uneasy feeling about Fanny. I told Grandma and she set me to memorizing another poem. I like memorizing poems but I am still anxious about Fanny.

Also there seems to be no newspaper to read here. I know Grandma gets *The Star* from Mr. Outram, who lives on the farm up the road. I saw one the day we arrived. But now, when I am wondering what is going on in the city, there is no newspaper. I will ask her outright tomorrow. Now I really suspect that Grandma is hiding them. That would mean the news was so bad she did not want me to read it. But knowing the truth is better than imagining the worst.

Then, tonight, she said she saw in the paper about women wearing "the Spanish veil" to ward off the Flu. It's a chiffon scarf, really. I asked her, "What paper?" and said I wished to read the news, but she said she had seen it at the neighbours'. It is so unsettling to look into your grandmother's face and know she is lying to you.

I hope Fan is all right. I'm beginning to feel even more uneasy about her.

Grandma also said people had been arrested for

coughing in public. If Theo hears, he'll be coughing like mad in the garden. He loves policemen, especially the ones on horseback.

Sunday, October 20, 1918

Pansy came in this morning, giggling, and recited the newest skipping rhyme to me.

I had a little bird.
Its name is Enza.
I opened up the window
And in flew Enza.

I was shocked but I had to laugh too. I don't think she understands it.

Even though today is Sunday, Jane, we didn't go to church. I asked Grandma if it was shut and she just shook her head and said she was taking no chances with her dear granddaughter.

Bedtime

I just overheard Grandy saying, "I think she has a right to be told." And then Grandma hushed him and shut the door so I couldn't hear another word. I am sure they meant me. What are they keeping from me? Something must be wrong at home.

Monday, October 21, 1918

No mail for me again except a note from Theo in Aunt's writing. It says, "I miss you and so does Hamlet. Can dogs get Flu?"

Why did he ask me that? Who would give Hamlet the Flu?

Tuesday, October 22, 1918

I keep reading to stop myself brooding. Grandma has a complete set of Charles Dickens books. The print is almost too small for me to make out but they feel wonderfully important. Father read *David Copperfield* aloud to us when Jo and Jemma were fifteen. He meant it for them but I got caught up in it and listened every night. Fanny sat there but she always fell asleep long before Father closed the book. Now I am reading *The Old Curiosity Shop* to myself. It is thinner and it is enthralling. The villain is much more evil than Wickham in *Pride and Prejudice*.

Oh, Fanny, write to me. Do it NOW!

Wednesday, October 23, 1918

Something is really wrong at home, Jane. I am certain of it. I wish you were real and here with me so I would have someone to talk to. Tim is not interested and Pansy is too young. I am positive Grandma knows something. I heard her talking on the phone. She always shouts through the mouthpiece as though she thinks her voice has to carry over all the miles with no help from the telephone wires.

She said, "I won't tell her. I think you are quite right. Let me know how she is."

After she hung up, I begged her to say why they had phoned and she pretended it was not Father but some friend of hers. Yet she keeps mopping her eyes. I cannot bear it. I feel in my bones — and in my heart too — it is something very bad and it is Fanny that has it. They say a twin knows when the other twin is in danger and I have known things before now. When Fan fell out of the apple tree, I dashed out of the house screaming her name until I saw her lying on the grass with her arm bending the wrong way. Oh, it doesn't matter about all the other times. I just do know when she is in trouble and she knows about me.

Right now, she needs me. Inside my head, I hear her calling my name. I must go. I must.

Fan is supposed to be at Aunt Jessica's, but I feel I should go home to our own house. I wish I could be allowed to make a long-distance telephone call but children never do. In my family, long distance is for emergencies. And they only talk for three minutes exactly because it is so expensive.

Still, I think I will try it. I can tell the operator our

number while Grandma is putting Pansy to bed.

I will do it, Jane, no matter what.

Bedtime

I tried, Jane. I had the number ready to say and when Grandma took Pansy upstairs, and Grandy and Tim were out in the cowshed, I took down the receiver from its hook. The operator said, "Number please." And, oh, Jane, I was so nervous that my voice came out all squeaky like a two-year-old's. There was this silence and then the woman said, "Little girl, does your mother know you are making a long-distance call?" I was so flustered I hung up. And I could not try again! It was too humiliating.

Then Grandma called down to ask who I was talking to. I said I was talking to myself, which was smart because I do. Grandma teases me about it. She says she has heard that it is the first sign that your mind is failing.

I could try to call again but I've been thinking it over. If I did get through, I would not know whether or not to believe them because I would not be able to see their faces. If Fanny is sick, they would want to keep me away so I would not catch whatever it is. I have to be there in person to find out.

So I have made up my mind to go. Now I just have to work out a good plan. The thought is a relief but it scares me half to death.

I am as sure as I can be that she is at home. I think I can get there by myself. I have already walked into Long Branch, twice, when Grandma has sent Tim and me to do errands. And I know where to catch the train. It will take me to the streetcar stop. Luckily it is not far into the city. Also, very luckily, I have the money Father gave me.

I am nervous but I must do it.

Grandma is going to her WMS meeting tomorrow afternoon and Tim and Pansy are going to stay at a neighbour's house until she comes home. They have two boys near Tim's age. I asked to stay here and will set out while they are all away. I can walk to town. I know the train goes every afternoon. I will just wait till it comes.

Thursday, October 24, 1918
On the train

I am on the train. I came out the front door with my bag and ran straight into Grandy. I thought he had gone into town with Grandma. I looked at him and he looked at me. Then he nodded at my bag.

"Are you going home, Fee?" he asked calmly. "If you are, I'll hitch up the horse and drive you to the depot."

I stood there with my mouth open and then I

came to my senses and dropped the bag long enough to hug him. He was back in no time, driving the gig. When we got to Long Branch, he helped me into the depot and bought me a ticket. I told him I thought I should go home to our own house and he nodded his head. I also tried to get him to take my money but he waved it away.

When the train came, he said, "You are right to go, young Fee. I believe they need you. You are sure you know the way?"

I nodded and here I am, safe on the train and on my way home. I feel brave, almost heroic. Swashbuckling? Not quite.

I am almost too nervous to write. But I am too nervous just to sit and think what is ahead. It is a good thing I take this diary with me wherever I go. Jane, you are a great comfort.

A man across the aisle keeps staring at me. Should I move? No. Why should I?

We will be there soon. Grandy will do his best to keep Grandma from getting upset. I wish I felt braver myself but it is good to be doing something.

On the streetcar

I am sitting beside Carrie Galt. She got on when we stopped at Mimico. I have never been so glad to see anybody. She was visiting her relations. She has not heard any news about Fanny but she has been in Mimico. Carrie says she will come with me all the way to Collier St. I am so grateful. I must stop trying to write about it all or I might burst into tears and distract her. She is studying a book called *Gray's Anatomy*. She keeps glaring at it. I think it is not her favourite subject.

Home

My bones were right. Fanny is here. She is alive but terribly ill. She got brought home from Aunt Jessica's a week or so ago because their son George caught the Flu and was sent home from university. We don't know how he is today. But Fanny got feverish a few days after she arrived home. Soon after that, she was burning up. Grandmother, who likes to make things sound as bad as possible, told me this and added that the doctor said fever was the first stage of the Flu. Next Fanny would start choking on phlegm and come down with pneumonia. "I am sorry to have to tell you this, Fiona, but you need to be prepared," she began. "There isn't much hope . . . "

I pushed her out of the way, Jane, and rushed up to our room. They said I must not go in but Fanny fixed that by calling out my name in a hoarse voice. I marched right past Aunt, who was doing her best to stop me in my tracks. I did not take time to think.

I just did what I knew I should.

The worst moment, almost, was when I came to her bedside and she did not know me. She stared at me with big glassy eyes and called out, "Fee. I need Fee."

I wanted to hug her but Aunt would not let me get close until I put on a mask. She wears one every time she goes near Fan. Of course, I did not look like myself in the mask, but at last she knew my voice and gripped my hands with her thin fingers. Oh, Jane, her pretty hands are like claws.

They tried to order me out but Fanny cried out for me again. It was terrible. She seemed to quiet a bit while I held her hands in mine. Aunt still tried to argue with me but she is too tired to do battle. Theo is not allowed even in the doorway of her room.

The doctor told us he thought Fanny was nearing the crisis. "It might be tonight," he said. "Once their faces . . . "

He did not finish but it was bad news, I could tell. Her face had turned a greyish colour. He sounded so like the doctor in *Little Women*, but this is not just a story.

Jane, I sit here in Fanny's room. I can hardly bear to look at her. She is grey and her breath rasps and gurgles and wheezes. She has lost pounds. Her face is all hollow and a dark colour. A bluish grey. That is one of the symptoms of this Flu, Aunt said. Nobody is saying the word but we all know. So many have died, but not my Fan. I will not leave her whatever anyone says. I am giving her some of my strength. I can't make them understand, Jane, but I must stay or she might leave me. I vow, here and now, that I will not let her go.

Later

Aunt wants me to come out for some fresh air.

I won't.

"Breathe, Fan," I order her, over and over. "Breathe."

I heard Grandmother, in the hall, telling Father that I was being morbid.

"How can you say such things, Mother?" he said. "If anyone can save her, it will be her sister."

So he knows. And he will back me up.

After supper

I could not eat even though Aunt carried up a tray. When she was not looking, I slipped the biscuits and cheese into my apron pocket and dumped the Horlicks out the window. I hope it rains and washes it off the window ledge before anyone notices.

Oh, Jane, I am writing to you because I cannot sit still unless I have something to do. Mostly I hold onto Fanny's hand but then she grows so restless and pushes me away. Whenever anyone comes near, though, she reaches for me again and clings for dear life. I feel as though I am made of glass and may fly apart into little sharp slivers.

After a break

Fanny is still alive. The doctor is coming back. Aunt has gone to make sure Theo is all right. Father is putting him to bed. Aunt just looks in and blows Theo kisses from the door. I saw her do it. She keeps her mask on the whole time. Theo asked how the kiss could get out and Aunt said a kiss can fly right around the world with no trouble.

Wearing that mask may do no good. Nobody knows how you catch this Flu. And nobody knows a cure. Yet Aunt can't take a chance. It is like the Plague in the olden days.

"Fanny, breathe," I tell her in my strongest voice. If she was not so sick she would tell me to stop being so bossy.

She must not guess how frightened I am.

3 a.m., Friday, October 25, 1918

I am so tired. But I must not sleep. I have a feeling that, if I can watch till morning breaks, my Fan will live.

But I am so tired and there is no sign yet that

morning is ever going to come. If only the sky would start to show a trace of light! I feel sure she will be better then. Must not fall asleep. I know it makes no sense. Stay awake, Fee. Watch

I fell asleep in my chair. I had been holding Fanny's hand lightly because it was so hot. I started to write and then the pen dropped from my grasp, leaving a smear of ink behind.

Fan's voice jerked me awake. "So dark," she said, suddenly, in a croaky mutter. "Why so dark?"

"The dark comes early now," I said. But she was gone again and did not hear me.

She is still alive though. I must not sleep again. I still can hardly believe I slept. But I remember that the disciples fell asleep when Jesus himself told them to stay awake. I used to think they were awful and I never understood that part until tonight. But they could not help it and neither could I. Fighting sleep is like trying not to sink into quicksand. It drags you down however you struggle against it.

I felt myself beginning to drift again and started singing under my breath to wake myself up. "Abide with me," I sang, "fast falls the eventide." I had to change songs quickly or I might have drowned Fan in my tears. But I cannot really sing anyway. I will walk up and down a bit and wash my face with cold water from the jug.

Still Friday, the 25th
Near dawn

I just went to the window and I am sure I am not dreaming when I say that the sky is beginning to grow light at last. Grey instead of black. I will watch until the sun rises. Keeping watch is all I can do right now.

Aunt comes and offers to take my place but I just shake my head and stay and she goes after a few minutes of standing looking at Fanny's poor face.

In the morning of the new day!

I am in Aunt's room. I have had a bowl of bread and milk and now I must tell of the miracle. Here is what happened, Jane.

I put down this book and walked up and down to keep from sleeping again. Then I went to the window for what felt like the hundredth time and I saw pink touch the sky. And then Fanny spoke.

"Oh, Fee," she said, "I'm tired, so tired."

I ran back to her and snatched up her hand. It was not burning hot. Fear made me shout. "It's the Flu, Fanny," I yelled at her. "You'll soon be better. It's just the Flu. It always makes people tired."

And she laughed. A croaky small chuckle. "Always? How does Fee know?" she asked.

"I just do," I could not stop shouting.

"Fee, breathe," she said and her hand squeezed mine ever so slightly and then went limp. It was suddenly much cooler too.

Even though my heart did not believe it, Jane, my mind told me her hand growing cold like that might mean she was dying. I opened my mouth to scream but, just before I let loose a shriek that would have brought down the house, Aunt came.

"Fee, what is it?" she asked and then she rushed across the room and put her hand on Fanny's forehead. Tears began to run down her cheeks.

I tried to ask outright if Fan had died but I could not make my voice work. I clutched Aunt's hand so hard it must have hurt her. She looked at me then and guessed my thoughts.

"She's asleep, goose," she said. Then she kissed me. I had my mask on crooked and the kiss landed on my hair.

"But her hand is so cool," I said, still fearful.

"Because her fever has broken," Aunt told me in a voice that sang. "Your sister is not going to die after all. You twins are as tough as a pair of old work boots."

And Jane, you know what I did? Just like Aunt, I began to bawl like a baby. And I knew, then and there, that if Fan had died, half of me would have died too. I never understood before how

I cannot write about it. There are no words for what I feel for Fanny and she for me. And I never guessed.

Later

Aunt picked up the diary from where it had slipped to the floor and made me leave Fanny at last and go to bed in her room. I went, Jane, because I knew Fan would be all right. I fell into bed and slept until a sunbeam tickled my eyelids. That is exactly how it felt. Then I saw that the light of full morning was streaming in through Aunt's window.

I jumped up, Jane, as you can imagine, and ran to check on Fan but Aunt sent me away again. She promised me that Fanny is fast asleep and past the crisis. I am worn out but blessedly happy. I must rest now or I may contract the disease and Fanny will be the one to keep vigil!!

She would too.

I hope I have two daughters, Jane, so you can have a sister. I cannot imagine what would have become of me without Fan. And to think I thought we were so different that we were not really so very close.

My cousin George's Flu, by the way, turned out to be a mild case, although they have not let him go back to the university yet. I was never worried about him, but I'm glad Father is relieved.

Bedtime

Fanny is so much better tonight. Ever since she could swallow again, I have had to spoon custards into her mouth. And make her mugs of Horlicks Malted Milk. It is supposed to be especially good for people who have had Influenza, according to Aunt.

I have only had a short time of serving the patient but I already feel great sympathy for those poor mother robins who fly back and forth, back and forth, bringing worm after worm after worm. But my sister is alive!

Sunday noon, October 27, 1918

There is no church service due to the Flu. Aunt went to the funeral of a woman in the congregation and found she was the only one there who was not a relative. And there were two small coffins in one of the rooms — two little brothers who had died. The funeral service was short. They told her they had had over a dozen in the last week. Aunt could hardly talk about it. It is like that bit in "Abide with Me" that says, "The darkness deepens . . . " But not in this house, not with Fanny recovering.

Fan is growing downright grouchy, grumbling about everything in a weak voice which is not hers. Nothing we do suits her. She wouldn't even drink the glass of hot milk Jo brought her, because it had a skin on the top. Aunt says that is a sure sign she is getting well. She told me she has seen this proved true over and over again. I hope Aunt knows what she is talking about. It may help me be patient with the crosspatch.

I admit to you, Jane, but nobody else, that I am close to becoming irritated with my beloved twin. She has been snatched out of the jaws of Death. The least she could do is act sweet and grateful for all the hours I spent in agony watching by her bedside. No, not Francesca! She tosses and turns and says the covers are too heavy or there are crumbs that make her itch or she is thirsty for COLD water. "Really cold this time, Fee," she whimpers, like that princess complaining about the pea under her heap of mattresses. I feel like telling her to her face that I am no lady-in-waiting and she is not a member of the royal family. But I remind myself that she nearly died, and chip some ice off the block in the icebox to make her highness's beverage cool enough to suit her.

I can't let myself look too long at her poor face, even when it is scowling so, because it is so thin and

I almost lost her and I do love her so, Jane. But I don't think it would be good for her if I let all that thankfulness pour out on her even though, like the 23rd Psalm says, "My cup runneth over."

I toyed with the thought of saying I am coming down with a fever or a sore throat, but it would frighten Aunt. Also it would be tempting fate. Thank heaven I feel jim-dandy.

Bedtime
Back in Aunt's room

I would not make a good nurse. That miserable sister told me so. Despite the chipped ice in her water. All because I spilled the water she was washing in down her neck. So terrible!!

And Jemma told Theo that there was a shortage of gravediggers because of the Flu. "If one of us gets sick, who will dig for us?" he asked, his eyes sparkling. He has not the faintest idea what it is all about.

"Go away, you little ghoul," I said.

And Aunt told me not to be unkind.

Maybe, Jane, I should see to it that you are an only child. There must be a way.

Monday, October 28, 1918

More waiting on Francesca! After a good night's sleep, I think I can be more patient. It is hard to be filled with loving kindness when you are so exhausted and anxious you think you may drop to the floor any minute. She remains as prickly as a porcupine. But I am eternally grateful she came back to me from that darkness.

I almost asked her what it was like in the valley of the shadow, but then, I couldn't. She is still so very thin and white with dark rings around her eyes.

Aunt and I have been taking turns sleeping in her bed and sitting with Fanny. But she says I can move back into our room today. Father set up a cot for me to sleep on. There is not much peace and quiet for diary keeping. Sorry, Jane.

They say that the epidemic is slowing down and, although there will still be some more ill with it, there won't be so many die. I pray this is true. We have been so lucky in our family. Fanny was so sick and some whole families died, but all the rest of us were spared.

The officials say we should cancel Hallowe'en parties. We were not planning a party but Theo wanted to dress up and go around the neighbourhood asking folks to shell out. Aunt and Father are still arguing over this. It is too bad. Theo isn't quite six. He shouldn't have to consider grown-up things.

Tuesday, October 29, 1918

This morning, Fanny asked me to sing to her. She's the one with the angelic voice, but I did my best. I sang her all of "Clementine" and "John Henry was a little baby" and "John Brown's body lies a-mouldering in the grave." When I started on "Danny Boy" she sighed and asked if I only knew songs about dying. I had no idea there were so many on the subject of death.

I was thinking hard when she said languidly, "You may cease singing until you can think of something cheerful."

So I searched my store of songs and sang her "Twinkle, Twinkle, Little Star." At least I made her laugh. That laugh, croaky as it was, sounded so good.

I then hit on "Coming Through the Rye." And she fell asleep, thank goodness.

It was wonderful to hear her laugh!

I can admit now that I was afraid she might die in spite of seeming to get better. But now I know she is really growing well. I could hear it when she laughed.

Wednesday, October 30, 1918

I am sitting in the back room in front of a small fire sipping a cup of Postum. Aunt thinks I have a sniffle and should cosset myself, so I am sitting here by the hearth. The fire is like a good companion. It chats to me but never minds if I do not answer. And, even though I like Fry's cocoa better than this Postum, it is still much better than a drink of water. Except on a hot summer day, of course. Then water is the perfect beverage.

The doctor is sure Fanny will fully recover but she is still very weak and pale and listless. I have never seen her be listless before. It is unsettling.

Theo is not going out for Hallowe'en. He was going to make a big fuss but Father took him off for a man-to-man talk. When Theo came out of the study, he had stiffened his spine and he held his head up but I saw his lips quiver. Poor Theo.

Hallowe'en Day, October 31, 1918

The paper said that the deaths for yesterday were down to only fifteen. As though fifteen is nothing.

I feel like spending the day in bed but I won't say so. It would terrify Aunt and she has been through enough.

Friday, November 1, 1918

Only two children came to the door. Last year they arrived in droves and Aunt used all our sugar making them fudge and taffy apples. The two who did show up were disappointed to get plain old barley sugar this year. Aunt let me answer the door, but I had to wear my mask and send them away without chattering.

I hate that mask. I even wear it when I take Hamlet for walks. Everyone else is too small, too sick or too busy. Of course, he could easily pull me over but he is a perfect gentleman and he gets so pleased when I fetch his leash down from its hook. Theo claims that Hamlet would be a perfect gentleman if he walked him, but Aunt has forbidden him to try. "Even a dog with a heart of gold can be tempted beyond his self-control," she says.

Saturday, November 2, 1918

The whole time Fanny was so sick, Miss Dulcie Trimmer never darkened our door, but now that the doctor has pronounced Fanny well again, that woman seems to be here every minute. She is supposed to be visiting Grandmother but she is forever to be found in the hall or the kitchen or just outside Father's study door. I told Fanny and she says she has noticed it, too.

"She lies in wait," says my sister. "I think she sees him as a catch."

If Fanny has hit the nail on the head and Dulcie Trimmer has her eye on Father, I see no need to worry. While she is here, he does not emerge. When he runs into her, he postively scuttles away and looks hunted. I told Fan and we laughed till we hurt. Aunt came in and asked what was so funny and I was about to tell her when I found I couldn't. I caught Fan's eye and she shook her head and told Aunt we were laughing over some joke that was not suitable for a lady of her advanced years to hear.

Sunday, November 3, 1918

I made the mistake of telling Father that I was bored and he gave me a pile of newspapers to read through. "Record some of it in your diary, Fiona," he said.

I told him it was the Sabbath and I was not supposed to work. But he just gave me the look that makes you hop to it.

I am NOT going to copy all that War news in here but it does sound as though we are winning at last. Just two days ago, our troops pounded the German lines at Valenciennes. It sounds as though they trounced them. And the end seems certain. Even the Huns cannot stand up to such a beating. We lost eighty men and a lot more were wounded, but if it means it will soon be over, I suppose it is worth it. I keep thinking of the wounded I saw with my own eyes and I feel sick. I wonder what has become of

Michael Franks. Maybe, someday, I will meet him on the street.

Monday, November 4, 1918

Nothing interesting happened all day long, Jane. Besides, I feel too tired to write. Nothing happening wears a young girl out.

Tuesday, November 5, 1918

I woke this morning to hear Theo chanting outside our bedroom door,

Remember, remember
the 5th of November.
Gunpowder, treason and plot.

I thought at first he had gone mad and then I did remember that it is Guy Fawkes Day and he wants to set off some fireworks. I wonder who put him up to it. Probably Jemma. She's looking for something to do these days. While her Normal School was closed, she helped with sick people some, but then Aunt decided she should stay home and Jemma was relieved. But she does hate being cooped up with nothing to do but help keep Theo entertained. I wonder if I could find some fireworks. I don't know where to look with so many shops being shut.

Maybe a campfire in the garden will do.

Jemma does not go to help the Sisters of Service the way I thought she would. Jo's the one who does it. Jemma says she liked the idea at first but she is not good at it. I know what she means, having sat with Fan. It is frightening and you have to keep changing sheets and wiping mouths and cleaning up messes in general. And you keep being afraid you'll be left alone with someone who will choose that moment to die.

Wednesday, November 6, 1918

Aunt decided that the whole house should be cleaned from attic to cellar so not one trace of a Flu germ will lurk anywhere. I have not had a moment to myself, Jane. Scrub, sweep, dust, shake and run up and down all day long. Pity the poor housewife.

I see to it that Theo does his fair share. Someday his wife will thank me.

Thursday, November 7, 1918

More housework. I feel positively grubby although we wash, of course. We scrub, as a matter of fact. Jemma says it is like working with the S.O.S. except, at least, you are doing it for your own people.

Friday, November 8, 1918

Jo has told us terrible stories. She and Carrie and their friends in Meds and lots of nursing students volunteered to help the Sisters of Service care for the victims, just as Jemma had at first.

There were so many corpses to transport late in October that there were no hearses big enough to carry them so they adapted streetcars. Jo saw one with ten dead bodies packed into it. Father knows a minister who conducted fourteen funerals in one day. It sounds like a nightmare but it is a fact.

When anyone gets started telling gruesome stories, I get nervous. Fanny was nearly bringing up her boots when Jo was telling some of the worst bits.

"Please, shut up, Josephine!" I hissed at her.

"Yes. Have mercy," Aunt put in.

I actually fetched a kidney basin at one point. Fan had made a choking noise and Jo laughed this new harsh laugh she has now and sang out, "Hasten, Jason! Bring the basin." Fan looked daggers at her but did not vomit. I was devoutly thankful. I'm fine until I smell it and then I can't help gagging. (Sorry, Jane, but you want to know ALL about your young mother, don't you?)

One family Jo and Carrie went to help had almost all died before they arrived. Only two little girls were alive, huddled up side by side in an upstairs room.

Downstairs lay their mother, their baby sister and their father, all stone dead.

I think Jo should not go near such a place, even if she is a Sister of Service. I am afraid for her. She is not sick but she looks tired and sort of haunted.

I had bad dreams after she told us about one visit. I think she is incredibly brave, but not her old loving self any more. I asked Aunt if she thought our Jo was growing hard. She said, "I know what you mean, Fee. But she has to make herself tough and keep her heart strong or she would be of no use. How could you face going into the next house after finding most of a family dead? What use would she be if she collapsed on the spot and sat weeping and wailing? She must fight down her true feelings daily."

I saw what she meant but it is still troubling to find my Jo a stranger. I am terrified she will catch the disease. But she says she somehow knows she and Carrie will come through as long as they keep giving their best. "Maybe being with people who are ill is lending us some kind of immunity," she said last night.

"You take care," Father snapped at her. Then, for the millionth time, he told her to wash her hands with carbolic soap and keep her mask on and get out in the fresh air every chance she got. And to give her aunt every stitch of her clothes the minute she came home so they can be washed. Jo laughed at him but she does what he told her. I know that the horrors she is facing must make her fearful inside, but she makes fun of our worries.

Jemma hooted when Father finished his speech this time. "You'll have her doing a striptease on the front verandah," she told him. "The neighbours will be calling the police and they'll cart Jo away stark naked before she can put her clean duds on."

"Jemima!" Grandmother shrieked. "Don't be vulgar. I never thought a granddaughter of mine would use such coarse language."

Father scowled at Jemma and then he must have guessed it was her fear for Jo that made her speak that way. That is what I think anyway. I thought over what she said, because she didn't swear, and it must have been the words "striptease" and "stark naked" that got Grandmother's goat. Jemma has nerve.

"Just see that you get clean," Father told Jo and stalked out of the room.

During the night

I woke with a nightmare, Jane, and I heard Jemma crying. I was going to go in to her but then I caught Aunt's voice through her door, talking gently. So I came back to bed. This is a strange time. Hardly anything feels ordinary. If we went back to school, that would help. But they are not opening the schools yet.

Saturday, November 9, 1918

Carrie and her brother William came over last night. She brought us a burnt leather cake, made with her own hands. We had never had such a thing before. It sounded dreadful but we discovered that, despite its name, it is a real delicacy. It was to celebrate Fanny's getting out of bed and joining the world again.

We were all so glad to see her back at her place at the table. Aunt told us not to wear her out.

Carrie said mournfully, "No games of Pounce, then?"

Everybody laughed but not one of us said, "Oh, yes! Let's play." We really are still not up to such jollification, as Aunt says. It is partly spending so much time shut up in the house. I've read so many books. I thought I never could grow tired of reading but I do so long to go to a movie or take a walk in the woods. Anything outside this stuffy house sounds blissful. A spin on Pegasus would be perfect. I would go if Fanny could come, but Aunt says she has to build up her strength first.

Anyway, it may still be dangerous. I keep hoping Jo is being careful. She has been sent, more than once, to help out in a household where the parents have caught the disease. She says she takes every precaution, but nobody knows for certain what will keep people safe. Jo says I am tough and she is more so. But still . . .

After they left, Jemma said, "William certainly appreciated that cake. He ate more than the rest of us put together."

He didn't really but everyone looked at the empty plate and laughed.

Then Jo said, not laughing, "He was in the trenches, you know, before he was invalided out. He says they never had enough to eat. After what he went through, you can't blame him for eating more than Theo."

Nobody was blaming him, Jane. We were just joking. But the way Jo leaped to his defence, I'm afraid she's fallen for him. If so, I do hope it's mutual. Jemma has lots of boys trailing after her, but Jo never has had.

Sunday, November 10, 1918

Father can't think of anything but the War news. He is absolutely sure that peace will come in a matter of days. I hope he is right but I still cannot imagine it.

Fanny and I went out in the garden today. She got cold soon and her knees wobbled so we came back in, but it was good to see roses in her cheeks. Theo came out with us and so did Hamlet, his face as mournful as ever, his rear end pleased as punch at being outside with the family.

Jemma's friend Phyllis is staying here tonight while her mother is busy nursing her grandfather. I am glad. Phyllis will keep Jemma from fretting about Jo. Fretting is not like Jemma. She gets restless and makes plans to run away to sea. At least, that is what I heard her telling Phyllis. Phyllis asked which sea she was heading for and Jemma said, "The sea where the seashell seller sells seashells."

Monday afternoon, November 11, 1918

THE WAR IS OVER! We were wakened by clanging church bells and sirens and people cheering. Old Mrs. Manders from next door came out on her upstairs balcony in her flannel dressing gown and sang, at the top of her lungs, the first and last verses of "Joy to the World." It was perfect, even though it was still dark out. Father went out to check what was happening and came back in with the glad tidings and a big grin I haven't seen for ages.

Jemma and Phyllis came down to breakfast in their nightgowns. As soon as they found out about the War being over, they pulled on their coats, grabbed some bread and jam and ran out onto the street to join in the celebration. They did not even go up and get properly dressed before they flew out the door. Aunt tried to haul them back but they were too crazy with happiness to listen. She ran after them though and pushed masks into their hands. They laughed harder than ever but they did put them on.

Then they vanished around the corner and Aunt came slowly in. She was scandalized and also afraid.

We have been warned that the Flu is probably passed from person to person somehow and we should stay home and keep out of crowds where there is danger of contagion.

But Jemma had on her mask as she went dancing up the street, pulling Phyllis after her. Not that Phyllis was dragging her feet! They are two giddy goats.

I longed to go, too, but I would not leave Fanny. Also I confess I was afraid. After all, I watched Fanny almost die. Jem knew it was happening but she was never allowed in the room so she didn't see just how close Fan was to death. She's seen others who were ill, of course, but it does not shock you in the same way.

We can hear celebration noises coming in the windows, church bells ringing, sirens blowing and noises like clanging cymbals and people shouting and singing. I know it is wonderful and it is a historic day but it still feels far away and not quite real. It has been going on for hours!

I wish Jemma would hurry up and come home. She's been gone for ages! Aunt looks sick. She keeps muttering, "She wasn't even properly dressed."

"But you made her put on her mask," I said at last.

"Yes," she said, staring at me as though she hardly knew me. "Yes. I did do that."

Early evening

Jemma and Phyllis did not come home until almost suppertime and they were both still happy but exhausted. They dropped into easy chairs in the front room and they said they had blisters from dancing and sore throats from singing "Rule, Britannia" and "It's a Long Way to Tipperary" and "Pack Up Your Troubles in Your Old Kit Bag." They said they kissed soldiers and sailors and just about anybody and got kissed back.

Grandmother glared at them and said their behaviour was scandalous. "It's hard to credit that you are two well-brought-up girls," she said.

But Father ignored her and kept staring at Jem in the strangest way. Then I figured out what he had seen. He was not worried about their scandalous behaviour. He had seen that Jemma's mask was gone.

Aunt was looking as shocked as he was. I could

tell she was beside herself with fear but I do not think either of the girls noticed.

Jemma stood up and began to go to the kitchen for a drink of water. She had kicked off her shoes but she was still limping badly.

"Was it worth it?" I asked her. "Your poor feet!"

She grinned at me and said it was superb. That is one of her favourite words at the moment. She added that I should have come with them.

She disappeared into the hall and Aunt whispered, "She had it on when she left."

"Had what on?" Grandmother snapped.

Aunt didn't answer so I said, "Her mask."

"Oh, I don't think they do much good," Phyllis said. "They got in the way. I think she shoved it in her coat pocket. That's where mine is."

Jemma hobbled back in and told us that the most enormous sailor stepped on her foot and then kissed her to make up for it.

"He looked just like John Barrymore, Fee," she said. "Honestly. All my toes feel crushed flat."

She sounded remarkably happy-go-lucky for a girl with a broken foot. She had risked her life and she seemed not to guess anything was wrong. On her way back to her chair, she bent and kissed Grandmother on the top of her head. Jane, she acted drunk with joy.

Nobody spoke to her about her mask. I suppose

they thought there was no point.

Phyllis's father came and took her away in their motor car while Theo, green with envy, watched with his nose pressed against the window. He is after Father to get us one but Father says he can walk to school, and the church and library are nearby, so why spend money on an automobile? Theo is working on a good answer.

Then Aunt chivvied Jemma into a hot bath, washed her hair for her and put her to bed. If being clean can keep you healthy, Jemma is safe as houses. There was half a cake of Ivory soap in the bathroom and it is gone! The coconut-oil-and-tar shampoo bottle is also practically empty. If I was a Flu bug, I'd fly away when I smelled that stuff. I guess it is the tar that makes it stink.

So, Jane, that was what happened to your relations on the day the War ended. It is a bit of history come to life for you. Jemma is still singing in her room although she sounds sleepy. Surely she will be all right.

Tuesday, November 12, 1918

We spent all day doing little household chores while we watched Jemma for signs of Flu. So far she seems as healthy as ever. Just tired from all her jubilation.

School is back but Aunt is keeping us home a while longer.

Wednesday, November 13, 1918

Jemma still seems all right although she has a bit of a cold. That is what Aunt is calling it anyway. She made Jem go to bed to get rested. You would be bound to catch a cold from somebody, what with all that kissing.

William G. dropped by and asked Jo to come out for a walk. She said she couldn't at first, but Aunt told her she owed it to William since he'd come all this way. She went then but she was not gone long. It is easy to see that, sweet as she is on William, she is more worried about Jemma.

Thursday, November 14, 1918

Jemma was not safe. Tonight Aunt is sure the slight cold she had yesterday is turning into the Flu. She is sick in bed with it and so, we hear, is Phyllis. Jemma does not seem nearly as sick as Fanny was, though, so I am sure she will recover. Phyllis is a thin, pale girl who gets a lot of colds. I think she is in more danger. Aunt keeps checking on how she is by telephone.

Theo trots around after Aunt saying she should give Jemma a cup of Horlicks but it is Theo who really loves it. He'll get it, Jane, never fear. He has Aunt wound around his little finger.

Aunt just took Jemma a mug of Horlicks and she

would not touch it. She has started to cough. Theo drank both his and hers.

Oh, Jane, writing this diary is not pure fun after all. I never knew life could be so joyful and so filled with anxiety and pain all at the same time. It makes me feel deeply confused. I thought that if you were good and went to church and said your prayers, God would look after you. Where is He? Did He watch, with me, by Fanny's bed, and did He save her? If He did, where has He gone now Jemma is getting so sick?

I'd like to talk it over with Father but he seems distant these days. Aunt says he is weighed down with sorrow. So many young people he taught have died. That is one of the bewildering things about this Influenza — it strikes not so much the old and weak but the young and strong. It seems so senseless.

But the War is over! I keep telling myself. Peacetime has come at last. As old Mrs. Manders sang out, joy to the world.

Saturday, November 16, 1918

Phyllis died last night. Jemma is much worse. From outside her door, you can hear her fighting for breath. The doctor sent a practical nurse to help Aunt even though he said, "By now, they are as scarce as hen's teeth." She brought a pneumonia jacket with her but she no sooner got it onto Jemma than she tore it off and grew so wild that they gave up on it. I am not allowed in her room, and Jo has been sleeping on the pull-out bed in the back room.

Aunt is pale and hardly speaks. She wears that mask all day even though Theo hates it. She looks as though she has seen a ghost.

Jemma has always been taller and stronger than Jo, we keep telling ourselves.

The doctor thinks maybe we should cut Jemma's hair because it could be harbouring the Influenza. We all know that she would not want her beautiful hair cut off. They do cut your hair off when you have scarlet fever. One of my friends had it and came back to school looking almost bald. But Aunt says to wait. Every night, since she was my age, Jemma has brushed it one hundred strokes without any nagging from Aunt.

Why am I telling you about hair-brushing when Phyllis has died? I think I am trying not to think.

It sounds as though Jemma is delirious or something. "Give me a drink!" she calls. Then she chokes on the mucus clogging her poor throat. Aunt tells us that she asks for water immediately after she has had some. Aunt also says Fanny was like this before I got home.

Mrs. Davis, the nurse, keeps shaking her head in a

doleful way. I wish she had never come. Although she does give Aunt a chance to catch forty winks. It is more like five winks. She can't rest with Jemma so ill.

Jemma will get better. She has to. Without her, Jo would be as heartsick as I would have been if Fanny had not come back to me.

Listen to me, God. Save our Jemma. In Jesus' name, Amen.

I will keep praying. But there must be so many prayers going up to God that I can't see how He can pay special attention to mine.

Sunday, November 17, 1918

No change. Jo started to go out to do her S.O.S. stint and then turned around and came back in. Aunt telephoned the Galts to tell them what was happening. Jo is in Aunt's bedroom now. I went up to see if I could help somehow but she just said, "Leave me alone, Fee. I'm better alone." So I did.

Monday, November 18, 1918

Jemma is still alive but she is now as sick as Fanny ever was. Aunt stays in the room with her and the doctor took his nurse away when Aunt told him she would rather be without her. When she needs anything, I take it to the door. They think I might be immune because of being with Fanny, but nobody really knows.

Oh, Jane, I cannot write any more about these days.

Tuesday, November 19, 1918

Jemma is no better. Even Theo has stopped smiling and Hamlet is so quiet. He just lies with his giant head on his paws and looks as though his heart is breaking. Pixie lies outside Aunt's door and will not be moved.

Maybe Jemma will pass the crisis tonight, like Fan. But when I said that through the door to Aunt, she didn't say a word.

The doctor told Father he should prepare himself for the worst. He said he had not seen a patient recover once their face became almost black like Jemma's. He shouldn't have said such a terrible thing. We can't give up hope, not while she is alive. Father looks like an old man.

Later

We are all just waiting. The whole house is filled with Jemma's terrible struggle to breathe. But we must still hope. I crept to the door and peeped in. I wish I had not. The girl I saw was not Jemma. Jemma had gone

I can't write it.

We must keep praying while she still breathes. That is what I heard Dr. Musgrave tell Father. But his voice held out no hope.

Wednesday, November 20, 1918

My sister Jemma is dead. She died just before dawn. Hamlet began to howl in the strangest way and then Aunt called to us to come.

At least we never cut off her beautiful hair.

I feel I cannot write about it. Yet I cannot keep so much pain shut up inside me.

Thursday, November 21, 1918

I don't know how Jo can bear it. Their room has been cleaned already even though it has not been two days. I asked why and Aunt said we must rid the house of any trace of the contagion.

She is right, of course. We must not endanger Theo — or Aunt herself. She has spent so much time exposed to whatever causes the disease. And she looks exhausted. It terrifies me to think of anything bad happening to her.

I think I will tell Father to make her lie down. She pays no attention to me but she would listen to him.

Later

Jo is in their bedroom alone. When I listen outside the door, there is only a terrible loud silence. If you think a silence cannot be loud, Jane, you are wrong. It slams against your ears.

Jo closed herself in there and when we knock, she makes no answer or, if we keep it up, she asks us to go away. I did as she said but I felt such pain for her. Then Theo walked to the door and simply opened it and went in. I waited but he did not come back out. Then I heard Jo start to cry and Theo saying, "Don't cry, Jo. Aunt says Jemma is all better now." His little voice was so clear and steady, sure of each word he spoke. I turned away, crying myself, Jane, and there was Aunt sitting on the top step of the stairs, leaning against the wall, with her eyes closed and tears making her face shine. I went to her and we held onto each other and felt comforted. Father did tell her to rest. I pulled her up from the stair step and led her to my bed. It is the quietest place at the moment. She collapsed and has not moved for over two hours.

Jemma's body has been taken away, of course. The funeral will be tomorrow. They said it was the fourth young person to die in the last twenty-four hours.

Carrie and William came to the door but Jo would not come down.

Bedtime

Why was Fanny saved and Jemma taken, Jane? I feel I must know and then I know I never will. How can anyone know? Could it be that Fan was stronger? She'd just been on a holiday while Jemma

Poor, poor Jo.

I wonder if Carrie thinks such things. After all, her older brother was killed but William was sent home. Does she wonder why it was William who was spared?

Friday, November 22, 1918

Because of the Flu, we did not have visitation ahead of the funeral. We stayed quietly at home this morning. Father's Sunday School boys are being pall-bearers even though Jemma did have the Flu. As it is, Charles is ill and Barclay has been sent to his grandparents' farm until all danger is past.

I sat with the rest of the family in the parlour this morning and thought of the words in the poem I memorized.

Twilight and evening bell,
And after that, the dark!
And may there be no sadness of farewell,
When I embark.

All I could think of was that there WAS terrible sadness of farewell in all the hearts in this house. In the poem, it sounds beautiful and peaceful. But it must have been written by somebody old. "After that, the dark" has such a lonely sound. And it makes me afraid.

I know that Death is not like that, Jane. So lovely and poetic. Jemma suffered so. She could not breathe.

After the funeral

Jemma's funeral is over, Jane, but I want to tell you about it. She would have been your aunt. I want to remember everything too for my own sake. In spite of the Flu, many people came to the church. Grandy and Grandma were there. A neighbour drove them in.

Aunt was so strong during the service, and then we began to sing Jemma's favourite hymn, "Lead, Kindly Light." When we came to, "The night is dark and I am far from home . . . " Aunt began to cry in great sobs. Jo was moving toward her but Father put his strong arm around her instead and held her close.

"Hold on, Rose," he said in the voice he uses to comfort me during bad storms. "Hold on, dear heart."

I was so glad I heard. Jemma would have been

glad too. I reached my hand out and took hold of Jo's and the two of us held onto each other tight until we had to sit down again. Jemma's hymn ends up not with darkness but with "angel faces" smiling. And, when we got to that bit, I suddenly knew that wherever Jemma is now, Mother is there, too. It made me cry even harder but those tears did not hurt so much.

I must go downstairs, Jane. People are coming. I hid for a few minutes before they arrived but I can't go on hiding.

Sent to my room for insolence

Jane, I am going to write it all down, not just because I want to remember it but to get it off my conscience. The truth is I ought to be ashamed of myself and I am not even sorry. But what a way to act.

After we sang the hymn, I turned my head and saw that Miss Trimmer at the back of the church. She was all in black like a crow, with a black veil even, so you could not see her properly, and she held a handkerchief with a black border up to her face.

I wanted to run back and push her out the door. What right had she to come here and watch us suffer?

I hid when we got home, as I told you, but afterwards, I went down and friends and neighbours had come to the house to share our sorrow. Aunt Jessica and Grandma took over serving food and Grandmother poured the tea from her silver tea service. Jo kept herself in the kitchen at first, putting things on plates. Then, all at once, she turned and ran back upstairs. Aunt saw her go and followed after her.

Before I tell you the rest, I want to tell you something that amazed me. People were swapping stories — mostly about Jemma and Jo when they were little girls and up to mischief — and laughing! I never knew before how good it feels to laugh when you are so sad. It is as if laughter and tears come from the same cupboard deep inside you and when you take one out, the other comes too. They are like twins!

I was thinking about this and feeling lonely so I went to find Father. I was standing next to him when Miss Trimmer came rushing over and murmured, "David, my poor dear, my heart goes out to you in your great loss."

I felt maybe I had been too hard on her but then she clutched his arm and added, "I was astonished that Rose permitted your poor little Jemima to go out in those crowds. I should think she will never forgive herself."

Father stiffened and jerked free. "Rose!" he cried out. "Fee, where is . . . ?"

"Upstairs," I said.

He wheeled away and ran up the whole flight, two steps at a time.

Miss Trimmer had lifted her veil up and she went red as a tomato. She glared after him before she remembered to jerk her veil back down. She tugged it so hard that it came loose at one side and she couldn't seem to fix it.

I laughed. I know, Jane. It was bad. But I could not help myself. Some laughs just burst out without being invited.

"Don't you laugh at me, girl!" she snapped. "Hasn't that precious aunt of yours taught you any manners?"

I was furious, Jane. I did not stop to think. "Yes. She taught me that personal remarks are not in good taste," I shot back.

I was marching away with my nose in the air when I overheard her mutter, "My, my, what a hoity-toity miss! Rose's doing, no doubt."

It was as though she had pulled a cork in me and let the devil out. I was hurting so. I whirled around and a stream of wicked words poured out of my mouth. "Why did you come? You're not a relation. Nobody wanted you here," I shouted. But, because my throat was tight and sore from crying, my shout was not as loud as I meant it to be, thank goodness.

Grandmother heard me, of course. I swear her ears are as sharp as a cat's. "Fiona Rose Macgregor, go to your room this instant," she rapped out. "Your father shall hear of this."

I ran up here. I have vowed not to let myself cry any more so I am writing it out for you instead, hoping to take some of the sting out.

Bedtime

I was sure I had disgraced the family, but then Fan came up and told me the people had all left. She also said that hardly anybody noticed what had happened because Theo chose that exact moment to make a grand entrance with the Prince of Denmark in tow. He does time things well, bless his heart.

While everyone was cooing over Hamlet or backing away fast, Miss Trimmer took herself off, huffing and puffing. Those are Fanny's words, not mine.

"Whatever you said surely upset her apple cart," said my sister with immense satisfaction. Then she plunked herself down beside me and waited to hear the whole story.

But, Jane, what does that woman matter when Jemma is not here any longer to laugh with us? Fanny and I sat and talked softly until I saw how weary she looked and I made her go to bed and neither of us went back downstairs.

When Aunt tiptoed in later she kissed us both, believing we were asleep. Then she stood and looked down at us for a long moment before she crept away. I watched her through my lashes. When she was gone, I tried to go to sleep. But I couldn't turn off all the thoughts churning inside me. So I decided to share them with you. As usual, you have helped me sort myself out.

I just yawned, so I'll stop. Good night, Jane.

Saturday, November 23, 1918

The world feels so empty and grey. The rain has made the last of the leaves fall so the trees seem to be grieving with us. I cannot imagine how we will manage to go on from here. We are not the same family any longer. It is like those soldiers I saw in the hospital who had had their legs cut off. They seemed lost and so do we. One of them said he supposed he was lucky, but he did not feel like himself without his leg. I barely took it in. But now I think I feel what he felt. Without Jemma we are not the Macgregor family I introduced you to when I began this diary. We are a different group of people.

This morning Theo asked me where Jemma had gone. I did not know how to answer. Then words just came from somewhere deep inside me. "Jemma has gone to be with Mother. Mother has her safe now."

He kissed me, which he hardly ever does these

days, and ran off and Aunt said softly, "That was well done, Fee. And I believe it is the truth."

I had not known she was in the room but I am glad she heard, because I was uncertain about it. We hugged each other and that hug let me step back from the terrible hurt. For a little while, life felt usual. I cannot explain this, Jane. And it didn't last. But remembering it gives me hope that the day will come when things will feel normal again.

Is longing for that day being untrue to Jemma somehow?

Sunday, November 24, 1918

Miss Trimmer took Grandmother to church. The rest of us stayed home. Grandmother said she would represent the family and accept people's condolences. Aunt made a face behind her back and went upstairs again.

But, Jane, I must tell you that Jemma's death has aged Grandmother. She used to march about. Now she totters. And steadies herself with chair backs. So she does care.

I tried to read but found myself going over and over the same page, not taking in any of the words.

We need Jemma here to buck us up. Jo especially, although she is keeping busy now with helping the sick. I think Carrie helps her a lot. She's sensible. I remember how I liked having her with me on the streetcar that day I came home to Fanny. William also shows up every so often, which helps. But Jo is locked in her sorrow. Jemma was like a key to the laughter inside them both and Jo does not know how to go forward alone. I know because I feel it too.

Monday, November 25, 1918

School was to open on Armistice Day but they put it off a day. We planned to go back today but we couldn't. Even if we felt ready in ourselves, we would make the other girls uncomfortable, I know. I have felt it myself. You don't know where to look or what to say. I took Hamlet around the block and got stopped twice and felt tongue-tied.

I asked Aunt what you should say when someone tells you how sorry they are for your sister's death. Poor Aunt. She looks so white and pinched. Gaunt. I don't think I have ever used that word before but it describes Aunt's face. She sighed and then smiled at me.

"Just say thank you and then go on to something else," she told me. "But, Fee, you will also have to offer sympathy to others in the days ahead. We are by no means the only bereaved family we know. You had better think about how you yourself will express sympathy to others."

I was horrified. But she is right. I am thinking. It will be so hard to speak about such a thing but I will try.

Tuesday night, November 26, 1918

Even food tastes flat and wrong these days.

Every mail brings letters and cards saying how sorry everyone is. Just as you begin to feel things might come right again, you have to read them. Some say horrible things. One said, "God needed your child more than you did and called her home to be with Him."

I felt like spitting on it. I would feel like spitting on God if I thought He really believed we didn't need Jemma. We need her so badly.

Wednesday, November 27, 1918

Theo is wolfing down a bowl of Big Six before he goes outside and trying to make up a rhyme about it. There's a contest with a money prize for the best one. All he has come up with is,

I wouldn't say "Nix"
To a bowl of Big Six.

Maybe I should help him. Let me see. Tricks. Mix. Fix. Sticks. Chicks. Hicks. Licks.

Do let me fix
A bowl of Big Six
With your morning Horlicks.
It's a marvellous mix!

I'll think it over.

There are still a few cases of people dying of the Flu, but not so many now. People talk about the soldiers coming home soon. Some families are planning big celebrations. But so many of us are not ready to celebrate. Maybe we never will be again.

But Carrie came to see us yesterday and looked at us and promised to bring William and both her sisters over soon for a rousing game of Pounce. I am really glad they are coming.

I wonder if William keeps remembering the terrible things he witnessed in Flanders. Carrie said once that he has bad dreams. They sleep next door to each other and she can hear him get up and pace the floor when he wakes.

Bedtime

They came and we played Pounce. Father won!!! Imagine that.

"Your father has hidden depths you young ones do not dream of," Aunt teased. And her eyes sparkled with laughter for the first time since Jemma's death.

Jo seemed more like herself. She tried not to keep gazing at William but she can't help herself. At least, that is what it looked like to me.

Thursday, November 28, 1918

Mrs. Manders invited me into her library to choose some books. We hardly know her, even though she lives so close, and I had no idea she had such shelves and shelves of books in her house in her own library. She calls it The Book Room.

I am so grateful to her and so glad to have some new stories. She has children's books as well as lots of others. I brought home *Eight Cousins* which I have already read but we don't have it. I also borrowed *At the Back of the North Wind* and *Rebecca of Sunnybrook Farm* and one book I picked out that I'd never heard of before. Mrs. Manders looked at it in my hand and said, "You'd better not let your grandmother catch you reading that one."

I think I shall read it first.

Jemma's friend Faith Fielding was there. I did not know she was Mrs. Manders's granddaughter. She said reading had helped her get through bad times. When I got home, I remembered that her brother was drowned a couple of years ago.

Just as I was leaving, she took hold of my hand and said, all in a rush, "I felt as though the sun went out when Jemma died. It's shining again now but it isn't as warm or as bright as it used to be, is it, Fee?"

I just shook my head. I cannot decide whether to tell Jo. I think I will wait. I know, because of almost losing Fanny, that she feels as though half of her is missing and she will never be whole again. I want to tell her I know, but even though I love her so much, I cannot speak of it quite yet.

Friday, November 29, 1918

I do not want to write even one word tonight. I feel like throwing this diary at the wall. I won't, Jane. I promise. But the point has gone out of everything we do. I could not even keep my mind on the book Grandmother would not want me reading.

Saturday, November 30, 1918

Today I met Jo on the stairs and I reached out and hugged her. "I know how it is, a little, because of nearly losing Fan — "

I got that far and she hugged me back. "I have thought of that. You are the only one," she said.

Then she went on up and I went down and I think we both felt better. A tiny bit.

Sunday, December 1, 1918

It is December and Christmas is coming but nobody in our house feels a smidgen of joy. Even Hamlet and Pixie still seem sorrowful. And Theo looks like a small, white-faced ghost.

Jemma was such a one for singing carols as she did housework. She knew all the verses. And she changed her voice for "Good King Wenceslas" until you shivered with that poor boy who was the page.

Hard as it is, Fan and I must put our heads together and think of ways to make Christmas a happy day for Theo. He's so little. He lost out on Hallowe'en, and Thanksgiving was not a bit real because it's the day we were sent away and only Theo was home with Father and Aunt and Grandmother. He must not be robbed of Christmas, too.

Monday, December 2, 1918

Today we went back to school. Fanny and I stuck together like glue and ran like rabbits when it was time to go home. Hardly anyone but Mr. Briggs spoke to us and, just as I thought, they all looked away. But we are not the only ones. I will have to find out who else is gone. Some are missing, but maybe they are ill now or sent away as we were.

Last night, I waited until Theo had fallen asleep and then I called a family meeting. I told them what

I thought about Christmas. I said I knew we did not feel like celebrating, but Theo is only five.

At first, nobody spoke. Then Father clapped his hands together and grinned at me. "What a great sister you are, Fee," he said. "You are positively inspired. Tell us what to do and we will all help."

I looked around at them and everyone, even Jo, was beaming, Jane. So we pledged ourselves to plan.

Tuesday, December 3, 1918

It was easier to think of planning than to come up with brilliant ideas. I am wracking my brain but it just sits there. After all, Theo has a dog and a set of soldiers and lots of books. I will keep thinking.

Fanny and I went together and bought Aunt some new leather gloves for seventy-nine cents. They are not all that expensive, thank goodness, since we want to get Theo something splendid and we do not have much spending money.

Would Theo want a goldfish, Jane? After all, he has Hamlet.

Would Aunt mind?

Not if Theo loves it!

Wednesday, December 4, 1918

Aunt made proper Christmas puddings today. She saved up the ingredients and Grandma sent things from the farm. The house smells entirely festive. Theo's eyes are beginning to shine.

Fanny thinks a goldfish would be perfect. We have not spoken to Aunt about it yet.

Later

Father got out the box of Christmas stories which he has collected and tonight he began to read Dickens's *A Christmas Carol.* I was supposed to be studying but I could not tear myself away. We thought Theo would fall asleep and then we would stop, but we only stopped when the last ghost was coming towards Scrooge. Theo was wide awake and his eyes were like saucers!

"It's not to be read aloud to a little boy just before he goes to bed," Father said. But he promised to go on tomorrow.

Thursday, December 5, 1918

It is bedtime and I am almost too tired to write, even to you, Jane. We have so much schoolwork to review because of all the time we missed.

Father is insisting we catch up. I am pretty sure others fathers are not making their sons and daughters work this hard, but there is no point in arguing with ours. I feel as though I am drowning in Mathematics and Geography, which I dislike. Father says

Geography is a wonderful subject and he made me read "Cargoes" by John Masefield. It is a great poem about cargoes from all over the world. It did NOT make me like Geography. The writer of our Geography text had not an ounce of poetry in his soul. His words trudge across the page. Boundaries, time lines, crops, industries, capital cities, seas, rivers and lakes. There is never anything lively to be said about any of them. I think Father should try writing a good geography book because when he tells you about the mountains in Tibet or the cathedrals in Europe or the Russian steppes, you can hardly bear not going to see. I wonder if he would consider such a thing.

Friday, December 6, 1918

Father says he has just the present picked out for Theo but he won't say what it is. He wants to surprise us all.

We finished Dickens and tomorrow Father has promised to read *The Other Wise Man* by Henry Van Dyke.

Saturday, December 7, 1918

Grandmother had a bunch of her WCTU ladies over, Miss Dulcie Trimmer among them, so Fan and I took Theo sledding. We stayed out all afternoon and came in with our teeth chattering and our noses bright pink. Aunt made us cocoa and we went to bed early. We entirely missed having to be polite to Miss D.T.

But, once she was gone, we came down in our nightclothes for the reading of our Christmas story.

Monday, December 9, 1918

I am sorry, Jane. I know I missed yesterday. But we are back attending church although we don't linger afterwards. Then, in the afternoon, there is Sunday School and we are rehearsing for the Christmas Concert. Then it is evening and we need to hear the Christmas stories. Father says those who do not study do not get stories. I do not think he would make us forfeit one, really, but I can't take the chance.

Last night he read "Why the Chimes Rang." I could tell Theo was pretending he was the Little Brother.

The rest of the day was filled with doing jobs for Aunt and keeping Theo out from under her feet.

Also, there are times when I need to go away by myself and remember Jemma. Otherwise it might feel as though I was forgetting she had been such a part of our family.

Tuesday, December 10, 1918

I am making Father read my choice of story tonight. I know he thinks it is "overly sentimental" but I don't care. It's *The Birds' Christmas Carol*. Have you read it yet, Jane? Carol Bird is a little sick girl and she dies at the end, but even so I still love the story. And it is funny in spots. Theo will love those bits. Even Father's voice grows husky when the angels come.

Wednesday, December 11, 1918

I was just going to start studying when Father gathered us all up — all but Aunt — and took us to the photographer to have our picture taken. Nobody asked him why because we all guessed. We have no family picture of us all together since we were small. He asked us not to say where we had been. Theo promised. He is good at keeping secrets.

Is Father giving Aunt the photograph for Christmas? He had a queer look on his face when the photographer got us all settled and looked us over.

"You have good-looking children, Mr. Macgregor," the man said.

"They'll do," Father said. But he had to clear his throat before he spoke.

Fanny says she saw Father blink back tears. I know how he felt.

Thursday, December 12, 1918

I am not in the right mood to write in this diary. I hate everybody tonight. I squabbled with Fanny, and Aunt lectured me about being self-centred. Be glad, Jane, that I am not telling you more.

Friday, December 13, 1918

It is all right, Jane. I have made peace with the world. Christmas is coming and the goose is getting fat.

I am not going to write down what Fanny and I have decided to give Theo, just in case somehow he glimpses my words. But it is a wonderful present. Oh, I did hint at it but it is more than I said.

Tonight we started on the Christmas part in *The Pickwick Papers*. Jemma loved that part. I can still hear her laughing at their trying to skate.

Saturday, December 14, 1918

Headache.
Can't write.

Sunday, December 15, 1918

Our Sunday School class is meeting again and we are putting on a performance of "The Cratchits' Christmas Dinner" at the concert. Aunt is still anxious about our going but Father says he thinks the danger is over.

I wish Miss Banks read as well as Father. I play the part of Martha, who hides behind the door when the father comes home. Ethel Maynard from Jo's class is Mrs. Cratchit. They moved to Canada from England two years ago and she still talks with a perfect English accent and she is also good at acting. Miss Banks was going to have us do a play based on "The Little Match Girl" but we said we wouldn't. It was far too sad. Tiny Tim is bad enough.

Thursday, December 19, 1918

We had a long discussion tonight about what sort of tree we should get for our Christmas tree. I hope it is decided to my satisfaction. I want a white pine. They don't prick you and they smell lovely. The others seemed to listen but one cannot be sure. Aunt is convinced all such trees should be firs.

Friday, December 20, 1918

Father and Fanny and Theo and I went to the country and got a Christmas tree. Theo chose it — an extremely prickly spruce. We set it up, with great difficulty, in a tub, with bricks to brace it and earth around it. We were so pleased that Theo began to dance about and sing "Jingle Bells." This actually inspired Hamlet to do his first, and I hope his last, prance . . . and down came the tree. Jane, you would not have believed the mess. It hit the piano, which made such a noise that Hamlet reared back and knocked over the little bookcase with ornaments on it.

The cheap ones survived. The one Royal Doulton shepherdess, who stood on top, will never herd sheep again. Theo howled and so did his dog.

"He didn't mean to do it," he kept roaring.

Tomorrow we are going to get another tree. We have to get another or Theo will spend Christmas comforting Hamlet who, he assures us, is heart-broken.

I think he probably does have some small bruises. He keeps trying to hide but he cannot find a big enough hiding place.

I wish I didn't keep thinking how Jemma would have laughed. I did not speak this thought but I think the rest thought it too.

Monday, December 23, 1918

The new tree is up and decorated. We put it in a corner fenced in with chairs. I must go and sing carols.

Tuesday, December 24, 1918

I did not tell you that our second tree is a white pine! Guess who chose it? I told Theo it would hurt

Hamlet less if it fell on him and the boy almost cried again. I did not mean to bring back painful memories!

The stockings are hung and Theo is trying his best to go to sleep to make the morning come. I remember doing the same thing when I was his age. He put out apples and carrots for the reindeer. He says everyone else leaves food for Santa Claus and he is sure the animals must be starving. After all, St. Nick has a warm coat, hat and boots.

What a funny little brother I have!

When Jemma was ten, she crept down and ate the sugar cookies Aunt had left out for Santa Claus. What a fuss there was when she got caught!

Happy Christmas Eve, Jane.

Wednesday, December 25, 1918
Christmas afternoon

We did it. Everyone knew it mattered. We found out, not long ago, that little Theodore David Macgregor had taught himself to read. Father gave him a set of the Book of Knowledge in its own bookcase for him to keep in his room. It is wonderful and Theo loves it. I do too. It is full of coloured pictures of butterflies and birds. The very things he loves.

Jo and Aunt bought him a globe of the world on a stand. It spins around and he loves it, too.

But Fanny and I gave him his favourite presents.

We bought him two goldfish in a big bowl with glass marbles to go in the bottom and coloured stones. We had done that much when Aunt brought home a china castle to go in the bowl. There is an archway the fish can swim through, too, and she found three more beautiful marbles that are transparent but wonderful blues and greens.

Theo was too overjoyed to speak when he beheld it all. He hugged everyone, even Hamlet.

Grandmother has been out at various parties and meetings so she was not in on the plans for Theo as much as the rest of us. When she saw his gifts, however, she went upstairs and brought down a coral brooch that is too big and heavy to pin on a dress. She had managed to get it loose from the metal clasp on the back of it. She said that coral had grown in the ocean and it would give the fish something nice to look at. It is beautiful, all carved with tiny flowers and leaves. She got an extra hug. I'm glad Fan and I chose an especially large bowl.

Theo still has a nap, or at least a "quiet time," after lunch, and he has put the bowl where he can lie and watch his new friends glide around and around.

Just before he feeds them, he rings a silver bell from our china cupboard and he is sure that Sunshine and Spot will soon know the bell is calling them to dinner. They are remarkably intelligent goldfish, Jane, as I am sure you have guessed. Fanny and I chose them because they had faces full of fishy wisdom. That is what we told Theo, anyway.

We all got lovely gifts. Father gave Jo a locket with a little miniature of Jemma in it. He had it ready. I think he had one of Jo for Jemma but he did not say so.

From Aunt, I got a great book called *The Shuttle* by the woman who wrote *The Secret Garden* and Father put Palgrave's *Golden Treasury* on my pillow. I love poems. I have thought of trying to write one. I think I might be able to if I put my mind to it.

Aunt's gloves fit her perfectly and she was so pleased.

William gave Jo a present but she would not show it to us.

Thursday, December 26, 1918
Boxing Day

We did have a happy family day yesterday and splendid gifts, but I made up my mind to tell the truth to you, Jane. So I confess that, except for watching Theo's excitement, this Christmas was really one of the saddest days of my whole life. We kept laughing and joking and being all excited, but Jemma's not being there left such a dark emptiness just underneath all the shining celebration. It was like walking across a wood floor and feeling confident it would hold you up and then finding a couple of boards had rotted away and you were on the edge of falling into a gaping hole.

I kept remembering how Jemma agreed with me about a white pine being the perfect Christmas tree.

Father kept shutting himself in his study, saying he had marking to do. He has never marked papers on Christmas before. Jo too was unlike herself. She would bury her face in Hamlet's neck whenever she didn't want us to see her tears.

It seems so wrong, so wicked that someone as beloved and good as my sister Jemma would be stolen away by an invisible enemy that crept in like a thief in the night.

I must stop, Jane, and go to sleep. I hope you never have a Christmas like ours — although it was also one of the best we have ever had. That sounds impossible. How could two such opposite feelings live in my heart together? Watching Theo's shining face worked the magic. The grieving made the day into a storm cloud but Theo was like the sun making the edge of the cloud gleam silver.

Sunday, December 29, 1918

We are beginning to laugh again. Hamlet is a blessing in that department. Talk about a tragic clown!

We were just cheering up when Uncle Walter came over. He started telling Father how terrible it is when people come into the drugstore begging him for a cure for a member of the family who has been stricken. There is no cure. But seemingly many people believe he has medicine that he hides away and only gives to his friends and family. Fan swore his face was wet with tears when he left.

"Nobody has ever mistrusted me before, Davey," I heard him say.

It is funny to hear Father called by such a little-boy name, especially since Uncle Walter is the younger brother. Father walked him out to his automobile. I watched the two of them and Father had his hand on Uncle Walter's shoulder all the way.

We are going back to sing to the soldiers tomorrow. I hope they enjoy it.

Monday, December 30, 1918

I wrote my first poem. It is very short. But it says what I was feeling as I wrote.

Why does the sun keep shining
When the world is so sad today?
The sky should be raining teardrops,
And the clouds should be darkest grey.
The birds should sit still in the treetops
And not keep joyfully winging.
Yet, sad as I am, I do believe
The children should go on singing.

I won't read anything in my *Golden Treasury* for a few days in case I see mine is too stupid to bear. I heard Theo singing "Jingle Bells" again and that started my writing it.

Tuesday, December 31, 1918
New Year's Eve

Really it is nearly one a.m. So I suppose it is technically New Year's Day already.

It is a good thing Father and Aunt are asleep and can't see our light. Neither of us can sleep so Fan is reading a chapter in her Christmas book while I tell about our evening.

Carrie and her sister Gerda took Jo and Fanny and me with them to Mimico to visit their cousins. Her uncle is the superintendent of the Boys Training School there and he has the jolliest family. There are six of them. It was wonderful. They barely knew Jemma so they did not remind us of our grief. We played Hearts this time but then we switched to Pounce instead. Everybody shrieks and laughs. I'll put the rules for it at the back of this journal, Jane, in case you want to teach it to your friends and I have forgotten how to play it. Even Jo got to laughing and then, all at once, she was weeping. Carrie's Aunt Jen took her into another room for a few minutes and then Jo came back, red-eyed but ready to play again.

It was like healing medicine, that game, and their big funny family. I hope we get asked back. None of them had been sick and the Flu is not nearly as bad any longer. It was the latest I have ever stayed out.

We knew we were not allowed to stay out too late, so at eleven we told ourselves we were somewhere in the world where it was already twelve and we sang "Auld Lang Syne." It was not easy, for we thought of Jemma and all the others who had gone from us, but the words held us up and we crossed our hands and sang lustily. Their Uncle George knew verses I'd never heard and I especially liked this one:

So gie me your hand, my bonnie dear,
And here's a hand o' mine.
Let's tak' a cup o' kindness yet
For the days o' auld lang syne.

I thought of Jemma and almost burst out crying until, all at once, their Aunt Jen saved the situation by coming with a broom and opening the door and sweeping out the old year. By the time we had finished drinking a toast of her raspberry vinegar, which was lovely, it really was midnight, but William was nowhere to be found. We were hunting for him when there was this thundering on the door knocker. Carrie ran to open it and William, with a silly hat on his head, bowed low. "God bless all in this house and gie ye a glad New Year," he said.

"And a glad New Year to you, laddie," their Uncle George said.

Then I remembered about First Footing. If the first foot to cross your doorsill is that of a dark-haired young man, you'll have good luck all the months ahead.

It was such a grand way to end the evening and start 1919.

"A year with no war," Jo said softly.

We had come by streetcar and shank's mare but one of the Galt cousins drove us home. We had a time packing all of us into their Model T Ford. There were three of us, plus William, Carrie and Betty Galt and the driver. Gerda took one look and said she would spend the night and come home in the morning. I would have had to sit on her knee, I think, so I was relieved. Jo ended up on William's knee and got teased. Every time we hit a bump in the road, Jo's head banged against the roof of the car. She said her brains felt positively scrambled by the time we reached Collier St. again.

Later on New Year's Day, 1919

Surely this year will be a happier one with the sorrows of war past and the Flu no longer taking so many lives.

For a while, people hung ribbons on their doors

to signal death had visited their house, a purple one for an old person, a grey one for an adult who was not old, and a white one for a child. Perhaps we should have hung one on our door when Jemma died, but Jo screamed at us not to do such a barbaric thing. So we didn't. Aunt drew down the blinds so the whole house was shadowed like our hearts.

But today is another day in another year and we are having roast goose for dinner and steamed carrot pudding with brown-sugar sauce. We never had it during the War. Grandmother will make hard sauce, too. You are supposed to choose between the two sauces but I like both and nobody can say a word against me since our mother always took both when she was alive.

We pulled crackers, too, with paper hats inside. Grandmother looked like Queen Victoria in her crown but she did smile when everyone licked their lips and praised her hard sauce to the skies.

Father proposed a toast as usual but it sounded so different this year. "To all our dear departed," he said and he had to clear his throat.

Thursday, January 2, 1919

I made a puzzling discovery this morning. Aunt and Grandmother had gone to visit neighbours whose father has died. It was not the Spanish Flu that killed him. He had a heart attack. I was being a good girl, the way I had resolved to be, and I was putting the clean clothes away. Usually I just carry them up and leave them on people's beds but I decided I could make an effort and fold them and put them away in the bureau drawers. When I was putting Aunt's clean petticoat in hers, my hand hit something hard and I dug it out. It was a picture of Father, taken long, long ago, and written across the bottom were these words:

> Rose, dear heart,
> This is to say I will love you,
> all my life long.
>> Your own, David

I backed up and let myself plop down on the edge of the bed. I still had the picture in both hands and I almost slid onto the floor. Then I just sat and stared at his young face. It was as though I was under a spell.

Jane, I could have been sitting there yet if I hadn't heard footsteps starting up the stairs. It wasn't Aunt but I leaped up like a scalded cat and shoved the picture back into its hiding place. I hope she can't tell by looking that somebody has seen it.

I came away into Fanny's and my room and threw myself down on our bed and tried and tried to puzzle out the meaning of what I had found.

What do you think, Jane? I was all set to ask Aunt when they came home and then, I knew I couldn't. She must have hidden it away in the drawer, where nobody would see, for a good reason. It was private. As Mother said, so long ago, it was not my business.

But it seems to say that my father was in love with my mother's sister when they were young. I've gone over the words dozens of times and it is as plain as a pikestaff, whatever a pikestaff is. I mean, he says it right out. He isn't hinting. He's practically yelling how much he loves her.

But if that is true, why did he marry Mother and leave Aunt to go off to teach in a one-room schoolhouse in Alberta?? Just thinking about it makes me feel queasy in my stomach. Did Mother know? I do not understand.

I must get to the bottom of it somehow but I will have to be careful. It isn't my business, after all. It was so long ago. He looks terribly young. Why did she keep the picture? I hope I put it back exactly the way she had it. I couldn't quite remember which way up it had been.

I'm guessing it must have something to do with those strange words Mother spoke, all those years ago, when I asked her why Aunt had never married.

It has to be part of it but it is baffling and I don't want to hurt anyone with my prying.

Sunday, January 5, 1919

We went to see a movie yesterday. It was marvellous. It had Mary Pickford in it. She is a Canadian,
Jane. I cannot imagine her living here. She is so
beautiful and she and Douglas Fairbanks make such
a handsome couple!

We saw an episode in *The Perils of Pauline,* too.
That girl is so intrepid and so silly and she is forever
escaping death by inches. I know it is ridiculous but
when she is tied to a railway track by the villain and
you hear the whistle of the train sounding in the distance, your heart thumps in spite of you. And then,
you have to wait a week!

I have not found out anything about that photograph. I keep watching Father and Aunt, but they
never give each other the kind of looks Mary Pic-
ford gives Douglas Fairbanks. They are old, of
course. Father is forty-five. Mother and Aunt were
twins so Aunt must be thirty-nine. I can't imagine
Father being in love with anyone. Well, maybe that
isn't true. But I can't imagine him writing words like
those on the photograph.

Jane, it is disturbing. I wish I had never found it.
Yet, at the same time, I am glad I did.

Epiphany

Monday, January 6, 1919

Last night was Twelfth Night. Today is Epiphany, the day the Wise Men came to give their gifts to the baby Jesus. Yesterday in church we sang "We Three Kings" and I wondered how they could tell that a star, high in the sky, was above the stable and not the sandal-maker's shop next door or the synagogue. I asked Father at lunch.

"That's my thinking daughter, Fee," he said, smiling his special smile at me. "I do so enjoy it when one of you shows a spark of intelligence."

They all laughed, all but Grandmother. "Don't be sacrilegious, Fiona. I should think your aunt would have raised you to respect the Good Book and the stories of our Saviour," she said.

Aunt gave a small chuckle, more a breath than a laugh. "I tried, Mrs. Macgregor," she said in a silky voice. "But her father's influence undid my best efforts."

Everyone but Grandmother burst into gales at this. Even Theo, who has no idea what was meant, giggled.

Nobody seemed to notice that Father had avoided answering my question.

I was annoyed at Grandmother for interrupting but Jo got revenge for me. She came into the front room where we were gathering, with a brown paper bag.

"What have you got there, girl?" our grandmother demanded.

"Buns," Jo said, sweet as honey. "Would you like to try one?"

"Well, thank you," said Grandmother and reached into the sack.

Jane, it wasn't buns; it was bones! Real ones — human!! Grandmother dropped it like a hot potato and Jo positively cackled.

Even Father was shocked at her glee. Jo had to put up with a lecture on the sanctity of human life but her eyes were sparkling all through it. When Grandmother finished, my big sister said calmly, "I'm going to get a skull next. Carrie already got hers — one with a crack in it because the woman had been murdered with an axe blade."

Grandmother had to be helped to her room. I longed for Jemma to have been there and I knew Jo felt the same. It wasn't funny, of course. It was Grandmother's spasm that made us helpless with laughter.

I wish I could put that photograph out of my mind for a couple of days. I feel haunted by it.

Tuesday, January 7, 1919

Theodore Roosevelt died yesterday. He used to be the President of the United States and people tell lots of stories about him. He led soldiers in a brave charge up some hill in the Spanish–American war and is the one Teddy bears are named after. Father was telling me Theodore Roosevelt's last words. He spoke to a negro servant and said, "Please, put out the light, James." I wish I could turn on the light for so many who did not die quietly like that, but choked to death from the Spanish Flu, like Jemma.

Bedtime

Oh, Jane, I don't know where to begin. Late this afternoon . . . No, I'll start at the beginning or it won't make sense. Theo and I were out in the front yard making a snowman. We had almost finished and I ran into the house to fetch some coal for eyes. Somebody had moved the coal scuttle so it took me a few minutes to find it. When I went back out, Theo had vanished.

He is not allowed to leave our property without asking. He's good about this. I looked all over the yard anyway. We don't have a large garden so that only took a minute. Then I looked up and down the street. Dusk was falling so it was not easy to see but I thought I spotted a little boy with a red striped scarf like his disappearing around the corner. There was a large lady dragging him by the hand.

I called to him and I thought he called, "Fee, help."

I ran like a deer and caught up with them on the next street. Theo was fighting to get away from the woman but she was strong and she was holding him in a grip like iron. Later we saw she had bruised his wrist.

"Come along, Frederick," she was shouting at him.

She sounded furious. I grabbed him and yelled at her, "This isn't Frederick. He's my brother Theodore. Let GO, you!"

She hung on and started to run but, even though he is small, Theo dragged his feet and he was too heavy for her to carry off.

Then I kicked her, Jane. I didn't know what else to do. My boot struck her on the ankle bone and she let go of Theo and doubled up. Then my little brother and I ran for home, Theo crying all the way.

But I did look back when I felt safe and the woman was sitting on the wall in front of Pearsons' house, weeping.

We ran for Aunt and told her what had happened and about the woman crying. Aunt went right away. Father went too. And they brought the woman back with them. She was still crying and making gulping noises that were not words.

Theo hid upstairs but I stayed where I could hear and see what would happen.

Aunt made her drink something and calmed her down until she could understand her. Her name is Mrs. Dutton and her young children — two girls and one boy called Frederick — had all died of Spanish Flu. I think Frederick's winter clothes must have looked like Theo's because, all at once, she was sure Frederick was not dead after all. Oh, Jane, it was pitiful. She does have one older daughter left who came to take her home. I was up with Theo by then so I did not see her. Her name is Olive and she said her father could talk to her mother and make her understand. But whenever he has to go to work she gets agitated and insists on going out to search for her missing children. They called the father at his work and he came to help Olive get her home.

"Poor soul," Aunt said when the door shut behind them. Theo raced down and flung himself into her arms then and she hugged him so hard he squeaked.

It is all over now but Theo says he'll never play in the front yard again. He's afraid she'll come back for him. I don't blame him. I saw such a desperate look on her face when I got him away.

The Spanish Flu is supposed to be over, but it isn't, not for the Duttons, not for us either, without

Jemma. It will always cast a shadow over us.

Close to one thousand people have died of the Flu in Toronto alone. Tonight all through this city there are all those families as broken and lonely as we are. At least, in war, you have a known enemy to face, but this disease is like a dark monster without a face and nobody knows how to slay it or how to lock the door so it cannot get in.

Wednesday, January 8, 1919

Last night, Theo had terrible dreams about being stolen away. He was crying in his sleep and Hamlet lay next to the bed and nobody could coax that great lump of a dog away.

"Leave him," Theo begged when he woke up. "He makes me feel safe."

Thursday, January 9, 1919

Stupid, dull day, Jane. Aunt told me I should not leave so much of the work to Fanny. She sounded tired but I am going to bed feeling like a worm. I don't like cleaning up messes and I do sometimes hide out with a book until Fan has the dishes washed or the beds made. Fanny enjoys those jobs — or that is what I tell myself. Maybe she doesn't.

I just want to be left alone!

Friday, January 10, 1919

This morning I heard Grandmother saying that they should not trust me with Theo, since I had allowed him to be stolen.

I ran into my room and cried and cried until I ended up having hysterics. Then Jo marched in and slapped my face!

"Stop it this minute, you selfish pig." She snapped out the words like more slaps. "It's hard enough for Aunt and Father without having to deal with melodramatic scenes from you. Nobody was watching him. It was as much Fan's and my fault as yours. Now get up off this bed and be helpful!"

So I did. Jane, do you suppose she'll whack her patients? She won't have a large practice if she tries.

I couldn't believe it when she smacked me like that. Nobody ever hits anybody in this family. What has come over us?

Almost noon
Saturday, January 11, 1919

I kept away from Jo this morning, Jane. And I did the breakfast dishes before anyone could ask. But I feel so strange. Not like Fee at all. What is wrong with me? I can't fix it and I can't bear it either. And you are not real. I probably will never have a daughter.

What if Jo should get the Flu? What if Aunt or Father catches it?

Bedtime

Today seemed long and dark and I wished I could run away to some other life. But Jo found me just before supper and pulled me out into the hall where nobody could see us and kissed me. She had tears in her eyes, Jane.

"It has been a horrid day, hasn't it, Fee?" she said. "I'm sorry. Your poor cheek. I couldn't seem to stop myself, but I am so ashamed."

And I felt sorry for her then and much better. I told her my cheek was fine and to stop worrying. I think it must all be because of coming so close to losing Fan and then really losing Jemma. It has been too much for us to bear.

Sunday, January 12, 1919

Theo is fine today. When we were in church, I felt like dropping to my knees and thanking God for his deliverance. Father caught my eye. I never knew before that he could read minds. When it was time to ask the blessing at noon, he said, "Let us give thanks to our heavenly Father that our son who was lost is found. And for his loving sister who raced to his rescue."

I felt some tightness inside me come unknotted. I took a huge breath and let it out in a whoosh. Then Aunt smiled across at me as we raised our heads.

"I do give thanks for you, Fee," she said softly. "I'm afraid I've been a bit hard on you lately but I could not face life without you."

I waited for Grandmother to say something nasty but she said not a single word. Amazing. Mind you, we were having shepherd's pie which she loves and she had taken her first big bite.

I guess I am still Fee Macgregor after all.

Monday, February 10, 1919

I know, Jane. I have written not a word for almost a month. When I swept under the bed and this book came out, I nearly stuck it somewhere out of sight and gave up on it. But then I thought of sharing it with you and made up my mind to start in again.

After I wrote the last bit, I thought I was over feeling queer but then, all at once, I just went to bed and stayed there. I was ill. No, not the Spanish Flu. I don't even know how to tell you about it. Father and I talked and he said he believed I became afraid of losing everyone after Fan so nearly died and then Jemma did die and then Theo came so close to being kidnapped and I overheard Grandmother saying to that Miss Trimmer something about someday Aunt would be leaving us. I didn't believe her but it all grew into a great weight somehow. All at once, I just could not keep doing everything I usually do.

I actually fainted and then I could not eat or sleep.

I think I was not alone in feeling this way. The doctor said I should go on a sea voyage the way they do in books, but he felt perhaps just a week or two staying home and resting would do the trick. The trouble was that, at the end of one week, I still could not make myself feel alive inside. I kept lying there staring at the wall. I didn't even want to read, Jane!

Aunt began the cure, I think. She came up to our bedroom one morning and said, "Up you get, Miss. I need help with the washing. Your sister has done it three times without complaining while you lay here not moving hand or foot and it is now high time you took your turn. If you don't stir your stumps, we'll have poor Fan going into a decline and I cannot manage all the work in this house by myself, even with Myrtle's help."

I felt furious. Nobody seemed to understand. But I rose from the bed and dragged myself downstairs and put the clothes to soak and started heating the water for the boiler and, all at once, the sun came out and flooded in through every window. Well, almost. And I knew that this terrible winter would end before long and we would have spring again.

179

Then I got busy and went to work with a will. When I had done my stint of housework and a bit more, I turned to my schoolbooks. I'm a month behind, so I had heaps and heaps of work to catch up. I could not take time off to write in this diary, Jane.

Then, just as I was beginning to feel like me again, Grandmother invited Miss Dulcie Trimmer over for supper and the evening. We got through the meal, although it was not easy, and then we decided to teach Aunt to play Pounce. We were out in the back room at the big table. Grandmother and Miss Trimmer were there too because we had a fire blazing in the fireplace and the rest of the house was chilly. But as we were in the thick of the game, the back door blew open.

Miss Trimmer shivered loudly and Grandmother said, "Fee, jump up and close that door. Our poor guest is sitting in a dreadful draught."

Well, Jane, our poor guest was not a cripple. She had nothing wrong with her legs or arms and I was winning the game, but Aunt shot me a look that said, "Just do it." I jumped up, ran over and slammed it with all my strength, so she would hear how I felt. But there is a frosted glass pane in that door and my hand and arm went right through it!

There I stood, with my hand out in a snowstorm, wondering what on earth to do.

Jo came on the run and helped me draw it back slowly. Blood was running down to my elbow from a cut on my wrist. A flap of skin had lifted right up and, although I did not know it at the time, the tendon had been cut.

Jo put on a tourniquet! So deftly that I was astounded. I was talking a blue streak and Jo sent Fan to get me a drink of water.

When she brought it, Dr. Jo gave me a pill to take with it. It might have been an aspirin. And when I tried to swallow it, my teeth clattered on the rim of the cup like castanets.

"What's the matter with her?" Fan asked.

Jo laughed. "She's in shock," she said. "It'll pass."

We borrowed Miss Trimmer's car and drove to the doctor's and he stitched me up. I had to have twelve stitches. And then he put a wooden splint on my arm and hand and bandaged it all the way from my elbow to just above my fingertips. I couldn't hold a pen or a fork properly. It was incredibly awkward.

It didn't hurt all that much until that night, when it began to throb. But I could not take off the splint for over a week and could not write for school or in this journal. It is unbelievably difficult when you are right-handed to have yourself trussed up that way. I longed to write all this down for you, Jane, but had to wait. My wrist is still sore, of course, but if I hold my hand just so I can manage now.

I am lucky to have Fanny for a twin when I am getting dressed or trying to cut my food. "You certainly are unhandy," she says.

That is all I can manage, Jane. Writing this much has taken almost two hours. Good night.

Tuesday, February 11, 1919

The cases of Spanish Flu are becoming few and far between now. They think it might have killed more people than the Great War did. I know that sounds impossible but Father says he believes it might have done so.

Carrie and I were talking the other day. I think Jo put her up to it. She told me about her brother Gord's death. And she said, "It is almost a year since he went on the Great Adventure." That is how she thinks of death. A great adventure. I did not know what to say.

"Did you tell Jo that?" I asked her at last.

She had. I think that might be why Jo asked her to talk with me. I poured out all my fears and she was so comforting. I told her that it would help if we knew what happened after death. And she shook her head and smiled at me. "I want to be surprised," she said.

After she and Jo went off, I felt a million times

better and ready to enter into everything again, I went to the kitchen and gave Aunt a hug and a kiss. She hugged me in return and said, "Oh, Fee, how wonderful to have you back!" Just as though I had really been away on that sea voyage.

Wednesday, February 12, 1919

Jo has started to talk about the Daffydil. It is a theatrical evening the Meds students put on every year. William is planning to go with her. I am happy she is happy. It is lovely to see her high-spirited again.

Friday, February 14, 1919

Pixie died in her sleep last night. We all miss her. It is surprising, since she belonged heart and soul to Aunt. But she would cock her head on one side and her little flat face would look so comical. She wagged her stumpy tail sometimes but often she just quivered it. It is hard to explain. More subtle than an out-and-out wag. When you were responsible for setting that tail quivering, you smiled and smiled. Hamlet seems to know she is gone somewhere he can't follow. He looks so sad and lonely.

Fan and I got valentines from nearly everyone at school. I got a lovely one from Ruby, nearly as pretty as the one I gave her. Theo turned our cards over

longingly so Jo and I made him one of his own —
Fanny had to do the cutting because of my sore
hand. It had a big red heart on the front pasted onto
a paper snowflake we had made, and behind that was
a sort of pocket holding an enormous sugar cookie.
He was pleased as punch. We had made a face on the
cookie with raisins and icing.

Then I made the mistake of telling them about a
girl in our class named Helga. She's a sort of refugee
from somewhere in Russia. She is so quiet and nobody knows her and so nobody sent her a valentine.
Theo felt SO sorry for her that he ran up the stairs
and got out his paintbox and made her a card then
and there. It was partly made of the one we made for
him but he crossed out his name and made a lovely
picture of a castle. It read, "Be my princess!" And he
signed it with a question mark. It was messy and I
was afraid Helga would feel insulted but I will take it
to her and hope for the best.

She has no family in Toronto. They live on a farm.
Her parents arrange for her to board with another
refugee family while she goes to school.

Lately, she has been following me around, for
some reason. She sticks to me as closely as my shadow — which is too close. She is forever putting her
arm around my shoulders or linking it through my
elbow.

I don't know what you would call it but there is a

certain distance around me that is mine and I only like my family coming inside the line. Maybe everybody feels this way. I am sure Aunt does. When Miss Trimmer comes at her with her hands outstretched, Aunt backs away and picks up a dishtowel or a cup that she can hold in front of herself like a shield. I don't know when I first noticed this. I don't know if she knows she is doing it. But it is what I want to do when I see Helga bearing down upon me.

What makes it most awkward is that she is jealous of Fan.

"Your sister sticks to you like glue, doesn't she?" she said with a sort of sneer today. "I am glad I do not have a sister who never leaves me alone for five minutes."

For a moment, I did not know how to answer and I almost pretended I had not heard. But I changed my mind and tried to change her thinking.

"We are identical twins," I said. "And that makes us share everything. It is mysterious, I know, and hard for people who are not twins to understand. We hatched from the same egg, after all. We become ill when we are separated."

It wasn't totally true but I had a feeling Helga might believe in it and back off a bit. I think she did. We shall see.

Goodnight, Jane.

The funniest thing happened today, Jane. Miss Dulcie Trimmer came over again "to visit Grandmother." She came into the hallway in her new wine-coloured coat with a fox fur wound around her neck. She also wore overshoes, of course, and a felt hat with a fancy plume. But my sweet little brother was mesmerized by that fox. It was a live fox once and it did look extremely lifelike even though it had glass eyes. I think Theo believed it was enchanted.

Anyway he stared and stared but nobody paid attention. This was a mistake, Jane. When Miss Trimmer was leaving, she went to get her fur and it was gone. We all helped search until, finally, Aunt called, "Theodore!"

He confessed at last. He had taken it to play with and he had made a true fox's lair for it in a hole in a snowbank in the back yard. When he fetched the fur in, it was wet and a bit muddy and looked as though it should be sent back down into its den where its vixen and their cubs would be waiting.

We struggled not to laugh. Then all laughter stopped when Father marched Theo into his study and spanked him. He does not believe in spanking children, but this was a special case. The neighbours must have heard my little brother howling. I hated that, but it didn't last long because Father hated it too.

Aunt started to sponge off the fox fur but Miss Trimmer snatched it away and stalked out the door. I hope she is so disgusted by what happened that she won't be back. I don't think this is at all likely though. She and Grandmother have become bosom friends.

I put Theo to bed tonight and he was still sniffling. I told him I knew Father could not have hurt him that badly and he looked up at me and said he wasn't crying about that.

"I am just so sad for that poor fox," he said, and his voice was trembling. "He loved the den I made for him. Oh, Fee, she is so cruel to him. She makes him bite his poor tail."

That is how the fur fastens, with the fox's mouth snapped onto the base of its tail. I felt sorry for that fox myself, by the time I'd listened to Theo.

Then he told me something I ought to have guessed. Before Miss T. missed her fox fur, she went into the bathroom to wash her hands. Theo did not realize she was in there and he opened the door just in time to see her putting her false teeth back in. "They come out, Fee," he said, his eyes wide. "They are all in a row on a pink thing."

"What did she say?" I asked.

"I didn't wait to hear," Theo said. "I don't think she heard me. I escaped with the speed of lightning."

I ought to have figured out that they were false. They are so big and whiter than anybody else's. I wish Theo had said, "What big teeth you have, Dulcie!" When I told Fan, we laughed and laughed.

Thursday, February 20, 1919

After they went to the Daffydil, William stopped coming around. Nobody quite understands why. But Jo is like a puppy who has lost the wag in its tail. William has sent no word. I think Jo has talked to Carrie but she does not know either, except there is a new girl going to the Student Christian Volunteer meetings.

"What's the matter with the boy?" Father said. He hates to see Jo upset.

Then my Aunt Rose reached out and patted his shoulder.

"It's all part of growing up, David. We had our disappointments ourselves and survived. They will, too. As we both know, even deep wounds heal."

She gave him the strangest look. That is what made me remember what they said. It seemed to mean more than just the words we all heard. As though they were speaking a secret language.

I sat there, watching them, trying to fathom it and not be noticed.

He looked back at her, as if he had forgotten

about Jo and Carrie. Jane, he looked like the young man in Aunt's picture.

"Wounds leave scars," he said in such a quiet voice. Then he turned away from us and went into his study without another word.

Is it just my imagination that there is something between them? I do not believe so. But there is nothing I can do about it, not until I learn more.

Friday, February 21, 1919

Last night, I had just written that much when our bedroom door opened and Aunt walked in. I shut my journal fast and I think I went red but if she noticed, she gave no sign. She just told me to stop writing and go to sleep, so I had to stop.

I wonder what Father meant by "Wounds leave scars." Does he have some hidden wound? Does Aunt know about it? She had a strange expression on her face after he walked out. I have not told Fanny about the photograph. I almost have a couple of times, but I decided to wait. I would have to confess to prying — even though it was by accident.

Saturday, February 22, 1919

I asked Aunt how you know when you are truly in love. I thought I was so clever. She laughed.

"Fiona Rose, you will know," she said. "You may

know more than once, but you will know. Now I want to hear your memory work."

She has always been good at changing the subject. But I love reciting memory work. This time it was a sonnet by Elizabeth Barrett Browning. It starts out, "How do I love thee? Let me count the ways . . . "

When I finished, Aunt wiped away two tears and laughed and told me I might be headed for the stage. Me and Sarah Bernhardt!

But were those tears really for Elizabeth Barrett Browning's love for Robert, or for Aunt's memory of Father?

Sunday, February 23, 1919

It was the Sabbath all day long and I will not tell you about it, Jane, or you will be as sick of being quiet and well-behaved as I was. When Miss Dulcie Trimmer happened by in the evening to "visit" with her dear friend, I came up here and wrote that much. Now I am going to sleep. Tomorrow will be better. At least it will not be the Sabbath.

Tuesday, February 25, 1919

Too much schoolwork to write in here yesterday but I MUST tell you about my discovery.

I was dusting the front room and I found a small, leather-bound copy of *Sonnets from the Portuguese* in

Aunt's chair, hidden under her mending. It was open at the very poem I memorized. I learned it from a school anthology and never knew we had this book in the house. When I picked it up, I saw this inscribed on the flyleaf, written in old, slightly faded writing: *For R. with love for always. From D.*

I was standing staring at it when I thought I heard her coming. I shoved it back out of sight. But it wasn't Aunt. It was Father. So, Jane, I pretended to be leaving the room and managed to push the mending to the floor as I went. I glanced back, Jane, and he was staring down at the book. I was longing to stay and ask questions but his face looked . . . looked like Theo's when he has had his feelings hurt. So I just kept going.

But, Jane, *R.* must mean Rose and *D.* must mean David, don't you agree?

Jo, by the way, went to a hockey game at school with another boy so I guess her heart is not permanently broken. She came home laughing at his jokes.

Wednesday, February 26, 1919

No new revelations. Just slushy old February. I long for spring. Miss Dulcie Trimmer does not let the weather keep her home though. She and Grandmother have started working on some quilting project together and she has to come by almost every day. Aunt tries to get out of inviting her to stay to eat with us but Grandmother just says, bold as brass, "I know Rose is hoping you will stay and have supper with us, Dulcie."

Poor Aunt. She tries protesting that it is not much of a supper but Miss Trimmer always says she will be happy with bread and butter. Then she trills with laughter — like Aunt Jessica's canary, Piccolo. It is a nice song when a canary sings it but not when it is supposed to be a merry laugh.

Thursday, February 27, 1919

I think and think about Father and Aunt and I make plans to find out more but my courage runs out at the last moment.

We are studying Shakespeare's soliloquies at school and Macbeth has my sympathy when he says that bit about, "If it were done when it is done, then 'twere well it were done quickly . . . " Something like that. I would like to rush at it and get it over with but I cannot.

I am waiting for one more moment of truth, Jane. What should I actually DO? Suppose the two of them stare at me blankly and say, "For heaven's sake, Fee, what are you going on about?" Then what would I say?

Friday, February 28, 1919

Went to the dentist today after being awake all night with a toothache. He pulled it and Theo told me to put it under my pillow for the fairies. I gave it to him. He wrote the fairies a letter telling them it was mine but I had given it to him. The fairies had better give him something. I must remind Aunt before I go upstairs.

Saturday, March 1, 1919

Theo got a bright silver ten-cent piece. Good for the fairies.

The troops are being sent home at last. It must seem queer to have the War end and yet not be properly over. Helga was saying that the older brother in the house where she lives is expected soon. While he has been overseas, his older sister died of the Flu. It will seem so terrible to him. At least, I think it will.

There will be a lot of families trying to live through such mixtures of joy and sorrow.

Later

Aunt sent me up to Father's room with some clean clothes that had been overlooked in the clothes basket. I made a startling discovery. I know I was poking my nose into things that are none of my business, but I can't help wondering about that picture in Aunt's bureau drawer. I was wandering about, looking at the books on his shelves. And I found, high up, a row of seven small diaries! I was just flipping through one dated 1898 and catching sight of the name *Rose* when Aunt called me to come and set the table for supper. I ran down and I stared at her and I almost asked her about the time when she was young, but I remembered what they had said about wounds. So I got out the knives and forks. But I did it all backwards.

"Fee, what were you thinking of?" she asked, pointing out my muddle.

"You would be amazed," I told her.

Jane, should I go back and read more?

No, I should not.

Will I go back? Of course I will.

But, Jane, if you ever find a diary of mine which I have not said you may read, Hands off.

I keep telling myself that it was more than twenty years ago so it should not bring the house down around our ears, whatever I decide to do.

I don't convince myself.

Sunday, March 2, 1919

You would be amazed how hard it is to go into Father's room and help myself to one of his journals and come out again without attracting attention. It seems impossible. I get right up to the door and then I hear him doing something in the room and I run like a rabbit. This has happened several times.

Since today was Sunday, everyone was home all day after church was over, which made it extra difficult.

Once I heard him coming and it was not him at all. It was Jo returning a book he had loaned her.

"Were you looking for me, Fee?" she asked.

"No," I said, stammering and going red right up to my hair. Then I fled, leaving her mystified. She has had her eye on me ever since.

Monday, March 3, 1919

Tonight Grandmother shocked and upset all of us. Halfway through dinner, Jane, she turned to Aunt and said, "Theodore will soon be off to school. What do you plan to do, Rose, when David no longer needs you? The girls are certainly old enough to take over the housekeeping. I think you've given up enough of your life to serve your sister's children, don't you?"

There was a frozen moment of utter silence. We were all struck dumb and we were all horrified. I was frightened, to tell the truth. I felt my breath catch and it was as though I was choking.

It was so strange. Father shot a look at Aunt and then stared down at his soup bowl as though he had been turned to stone. It was up to him to speak but he said not one word.

Aunt made a queer little noise, like a hiccough. Then she said, "The girls are a great help to me right now, Mrs. Macgregor. But Theodore is not even in school. I have made no plans yet. Please excuse me."

She did not run out of the room but I could tell she wanted to. She simply rose and walked out to the kitchen as though she was getting the pudding but she did not come back.

"She can't leave us!" I shouted at my grandmother. I made the shout loud enough to break through to my father, too, where he sat silent as a stick of wood. It is the first time I have ever longed to hit him.

"No, she can't," Fan put in, joining in breaking through.

And Jo said something cutting to our grandmother, something I did not catch.

Jane, I say I shouted at her. It was really a shriek. And I am scared of Grandmother most of the time, even though I never admit it.

But Father only got up at last to leave the room. He had not finished his soup. Theo pointed this out but nobody paid him any mind. Father's back was ramrod straight but he went on not saying anything.

Tuesday, March 4, 1919

We were sent to bed and I could not finish, but here is the rest of the story of what happened last night. Remember that I had said Aunt could not leave us.

Grandmother pinned me to my chair with her needling look and started in. "Fiona, consider how selfish you are being," she said in her voice of sugar and ice. "Your aunt is not an old woman like me. She has a good many years in which to make a home of her own."

We heard Aunt go upstairs. Father had gone to his study and closed the door behind him. With a bang that said something. But nobody knew what.

If I had shut it that way, Jane, they would have said I "slammed" it and ordered me to come back and shut it properly. Nobody called to him to do any such thing.

Then Theo, who did not understand anything except that Aunt was unhappy, jumped up, knocking over his chair, and scampered straight up the stairs to the room the two of them share.

"Mama, don't!" we heard him cry out.

Then we heard that door close, too. Another sharp bang.

At that point Grandmother barked at the rest of us, "You girls stay right where you are. You are not done and you have not been excused."

We sat still as tombstones, Jane, all of us silently hating her but not one of us knowing what to do about it.

It was dreadful.

Grandmother went the colour of stewed rhubarb and read us a lecture on being insolent to our elders. She finished off by saying, "It is high time somebody took you children in hand. Josephine thinks herself a grown woman, I can see, but you two and Theo should have some proper behaviour dinned into you before it is too late. I'm not the only one who thinks you are disrespectful. Your manners are disgraceful. Miss Trimmer and I have discussed the problem often and I am sorry, but I will have to do a little plain speaking to my son."

And all I could picture, hearing her, was that Miss Trimmer with her big toothy smile which reminded me of a crocodile. I could not forget the way Grandmother had acted. She had said something that day in the tea shop, something that made no sense to me when I heard it. I ransacked my brain until the words came back to me and now they seemed clear as crystal: "Give me time, Dulcie my dear, to clear the way for you."

Could she possibly have meant what I am imagining she did? If I am right, she is wicked. I also think she is crazy. I cannot believe Aunt would ever leave us. Nor would Father turn to Dulcie Trimmer for comfort, even if Aunt did desert us. He never would do such a brainless thing. Why would he want help from Dulcie Trimmer to make us behave? If Grandmother left, I realized, we would behave just fine. But what if she did not leave? What if she somehow caught him in her Trimmer trap?

I will have to do something drastic. I will have to save the day. Why me? Because I think I am the only one who knows most of the story. But how, Jane? I wish you were here to give me some good advice. And some gumption. Fan is a little too soft-hearted and biddable to be a perfect plotter.

Aunt's picture is the only thing I can think of. And perhaps something from one of Father's diaries. If I fetched the picture down . . . But do I dare? Oh, Jane, help me find the way out of this tangle. Tomorrow I will go and look, even if I do get caught doing it.

Wednesday, March 5, 1919
After everyone is asleep

Jane, I did it.

I know what happened now. I had to lie to get my chance. When it was time for Prayer Meeting, I said, "My head aches and I have a pain in my stomach." I knew Aunt would believe me. I started bleeding two months ago. Fan started a week later. Trust my twin to keep up to me in every way possible.

Jo had gone off with Miss Banks's Sunday School class and Aunt had to put Theo to bed and she had a book to read. Fan accompanied Grandmother and Father to Prayer Meeting.

The minute I knew they were all out of the way, I sprang up from my bed and pain and went, bold as brass, straight into Father's room and pulled down the book. I found the right volume at once by sheer luck. I opened it to a page that began, *I have made a terrible mistake.*

I am not going to copy it all out, but it is like a novel. Father told Aunt Rose he was in love with the two of them and he could not decide which one to marry. He was half teasing, half trying out the idea on her. She answered in a cool voice that he would have to decide for himself, but she could tell him right then that she had no interest in marrying any man who didn't know his own mind.

He was so stupid.

"All right," he said. "I'll propose to Ruth first and see what she has to say."

"You do that, David," said my Aunt Rose.

He met my mother later that day and blurted out, "How would you feel if I were to ask you to marry me, Ruth?"

And she threw her arms around his neck and said, "I've been longing for you to speak. Yes, yes, yes,

David. I will love to marry you."

He did not know what to do. She was so over-joyed. She said she must go right away to tell her sister. He could not stop her. And Rose said she was happy for her sister.

Father managed to get Rose away by herself a couple of days later and he started to explain. He said he had really known all along that she was the one he loved. But she refused him. She could not break Ruth's heart, she told him. And if he broke his engagement to Ruth, she said, he would end by losing them both. I wonder, might Mother have already hinted to Aunt that she was sweet on David Macgregor, so that clinched it?

She made him promise never to tell Ruth and never to speak of it to her again, either. Poor Father. I don't know why they didn't straighten it out after Mother died but I think I can guess. By then, he had grown to love my mother. I know he loved her by the time I can remember them. He has told us of her so tenderly. And Aunt was keeping house for him. And we were all grieving.

Wounds leave scars. They do shrink as time passes but they are there long after the healing is done. He wrote those words in the book. I must put it back and watch for the right moment. I cannot believe he is so slow that he does not know that Aunt still cares for him. I cannot believe that he will let her go again.

Friday, March 7, 1919

I have not been able to write to you because I have thought about nothing but Father and Aunt and Mother for two days and I have decided what to do. I'll do it tonight when we are in bed and the house is quiet.

I am going right now. Wish me luck.

I did it. I ran down in my bare feet and put Aunt's picture of Father under his pillow with a note saying where I had found it and asking why he did not reread his journal and telling him which date to look up. Then I wrote that I was sure she would not say no this time and if he didn't have courage, he might lose her yet.

Then I tore back up to bed and am scrawling these few words before I try to go to sleep. I might never sleep again. Fanny is beside herself with curiosity. I just told her that the suffragettes had set me a good example and I had done something brave. Now I will pretend to go right to sleep.

I wonder if he will speak to me at breakfast.

Saturday, March 8, 1919

He did not speak to me. He came in late, looked around at us, walked over to me and kissed me on top of the head. Then he picked up a piece of toast and left for some meeting or other. I thought I would explode.

Later

I waited all day for him to say something but he never did. What have I done? Have I wrecked everything? Will they forgive me if I have?

Sunday, March 9, 1919

Aunt caught me in the upstairs hall and gave me a big hug and whispered, "You are the best thing that has ever happened to me, Fiona Rose."

"What?" I said, sounding absolutely brainless.

"Be patient a little longer, honey," she murmured and whisked away. And that was all.

Monday, March 10, 1919

I feel as though I might drop over dead in my tracks if this goes on. I am not good at waiting.

Tuesday, March 11, 1919

Still waiting. I cannot bear it.

Wednesday, March 12, 1919

I don't need to keep biting my fingernails. To-night, when Grandmother had gone over to Miss

Trimmer's house to play whist, Father called us into his study and told us he and Aunt were getting married on Saturday!

They were waiting to tell us until Grandmother was out, Father said, "so your rumpus won't upset the apple cart."

They are being married in Bloor St. Church at half past ten in the morning and we are all to come. Just us. Jo, Fan, Theo and me! No Grandmother. She doesn't even know.

"She'll be at the wedding lunch when we get home," he said. "But she would not enjoy the ceremony. Your aunt and I don't want anybody present who is not glad we are getting married. Oh, Dr. Musgrave and Miss Banks are coming as witnesses."

"Is it a secret?" Theo asked, his eyes huge and bright as stars.

Theo catches on fast.

Father said it was a secret until we got home from church.

"Then will Mama be my real mother and not my aunt-mother?" Theo asked. As I said, he catches on.

"I will indeed, my boy," Aunt said.

She sounded as if she was choking over a lump in her throat. She says we girls can go right on calling her Aunt — she would feel uncomfortable if we all tried to change over.

Jo asked what she was going to wear and we left

Father in his study to go look over her wardrobe. She decided, at last, that she would wear her green wool suit. It is nice but she has had it for three years. Jo said she would do no such thing and went digging in the big chest our great-grandmother had and she found a wonderful old wedding dress in there. It is ivory satin with lace around the wrists and a deep ruffle at the hem. Aunt went pink and said it was Mother's dress and she truly would not feel like herself if she wore it. We started to argue and then I saw we were making her miserable. Jo must have seen it at the same moment. She bundled the wedding finery back into the cedar chest and gave Aunt a hug.

"You look like spring in that suit," she said. "I know Father likes it. You can see it in the way he looks at you."

I am not so sure about that. I don't think our father notices clothes at all. Aunt laughed out loud and kissed Jo.

"You are a dear, Josephine Macgregor," she said.

Then she blew her nose and Jo took the green wool suit away to press it. We are going to get her a bouquet. We are not sure what flowers will be available but they always seem to have roses. Too bad we can't pick her some lily-of-the-valley. She is as partial to them as Mother was.

Thursday, March 13, 1919

I just disobeyed my father and did a brave act, Jane, and my hand is shaking so hard that I can hardly write. Everyone was either out or in bed but me. This hardly ever happens in our house and, all of a sudden, I was inspired. I MADE A LONG-DISTANCE TELEPHONE CALL! I used my deepest voice and I practised ahead of time. I got Grandy. Grandma was already in bed. I told him about the wedding. I thought they ought to know. When I asked Aunt about them yesterday, she said she and Father thought it was not fair to tell one grandmother and not the other. Besides it was too far for them to come. She and Father would go and visit afterwards.

But I decided it was not fair to let Grandmother's meanness steal Grandma and Grandy's joy.

I could hardly believe it when the call went through easy as pie and I heard Grandy's voice. I gabbled out the news and he listened without making a sound. Then, when I stopped blathering, he laughed.

"Thank you, Fiona Rose," he said. "It is wonderful news. I will tell your grandma. She's in bed but I'll go right up."

"They're not telling Grandmother until after the wedding," I said.

"Well done," he said and hung up.

Am I in deep trouble, Jane? I wouldn't be surprised.

But I can't feel too terrible. I just looked out through the glass in the front door and Jo and William Galt are out there holding hands.

Saturday, March 15, 1919

Jane, I have only a few blank pages left in this book. I should have written smaller but Father has already promised to buy me another.

Father and Aunt were married this morning. It was quiet and private and so beautiful that I cried and cried. Theo got so worried that he said, right out loud, "I thought you loved my mama."

"Oh, I do," I sobbed. And everyone laughed, even the minister.

When we arrived home after the wedding, Grandmother was watching for us at the front door. Father had just left a note saying we would all be home for lunch. She must have been wondering where on earth we had all gone.

And hear this, Jane. As we got out of the car, a taxi pulled up with Grandma and Grandy inside.

Grandma got out and rushed straight over to Grandmother and did her best to hug her.

"I came to support you, Dorcas, since neither of us was invited to the wedding," she said, grinning at me over Grandmother's shoulder. I looked at Grandy and he winked.

Grandmother went stiff as a bolster. Her face turned purple and she could not utter a word. Then she actually began to cry. I wanted to hit her, Jane. I thought she was going to ruin everything.

But Father kissed her and then Aunt did, too, and she mopped her face and remembered her manners.

"I pray you will both be very happy," she got out in a starchy voice. "But we needn't stand out here for the neighbours to gawk at. Come into the house, all of you."

I felt almost sorry for her at that moment. After all, Jane, it isn't her house.

We crowded into the sitting room. And Grandma walked over to the piano and, still wearing her hat, sat down and began to play Beethoven's "Song of Joy."

It was perfect.

Sunday, March 16, 1919

So that is the story of the big day. What excitement!

Nothing much has changed in our house, but it feels different. Grandmother stays in her room more or is out with Miss Trimmer, as though she cannot bear the sight of Father and Aunt gazing blissfully at each other. Maybe they don't do that, exactly, but almost.

Saturday, March 22, 1919

I saved the last three pages until I had something good to finish with. Nothing happened all week, but today I have a great story to finish off with, Jane. And some good news, too.

The entire family was sitting on the front verandah. It was chilly but the sun was bright, perhaps to celebrate spring having really arrived. Father and Aunt were in the swing, holding hands as bold as brass, and the rest of us here and there. Everything was thawing and the birds were singing their heads off and it was peaceful.

Suddenly Theo sprang up like a jack-in-the-box and backed against the house wall with his hands gripped together behind him. He looked horrified.

"What on earth . . . ?" Father began.

Then we followed Theo's gaze and there was Miss Dulcie Trimmer, her cheeks very red, coming to call for Grandmother to go to a WCTU meeting. She had on a new hat, very big, with a wide brim. And, perched on the crown, was the sweetest little jenny wren. It was stuffed, of course, but it looked so lifelike and it seemed to be gazing straight at my horrified little brother.

"I won't," Theo said.

But we all knew how badly he wanted to snatch that tiny stuffed bird off her prison of a hat and set it free to fly. The fox fur had not been alive either but, for Theo, it came to life and made itself a den in the snow. The bird could be set on a twig with a grassy cup of a nest made for it by a loving little boy. But he remembered the shock of being spanked by his father who did not believe in "corporal punishment." The next minute, we had begun to laugh. Father himself started, reaching out a long arm to pull Theo onto his knee. Within seconds, we were all in whoops. I thought of Jemma, but only to wish she could be there to enjoy the fun.

Grandmother glared at us and stiffened to her full height. Her chest puffed out like a pouter pigeon. Her hair grew bigger and her glasses flashed. Then she made a speech, informing us that Miss Trimmer had invited her to come and live with her in her little house.

"We see eye to eye about so many things," she said. Her fierce look made it clear that none of us had managed this feat.

"I've left my bags packed in my room, David," she said. "I trust you will bring them over this evening. We can make arrangements for my furniture."

It was just like the day she arrived.

"Of course I will, Mother," Father said, sounding stunned.

Then the two women marched down the walk to Dulcie Trimmer's Model T. Their backs were poker straight. They looked like Christian soldiers marching off to war.

I cannot believe it. Grandmother is actually leaving us!

As the car coughed and snorted away, we burst into laughter again. It was different, though. It was like a trumpet blowing "Freedom!" It rang out farewell to the War, goodbye to the Spanish Flu, and so long to Grandmother's trying to take us over. Having her occupying our home was hard on everybody. Having her come for dinner is no trouble at all!

Now the day is over. But inside, Jane, I am still listening to that trumpet call and laughing. I thought I would never laugh again, but I was wrong. It feels as though tomorrow I will wake up to a new morning, shining with hope and happiness. And someday, when you and I sit together, reading my words, we will laugh together and maybe cry a little at all the memories of my thirteenth year when my sister Jo started medical school and the Spanish Flu took Jemma from us and the War ended and Father and Aunt were married and your Uncle Theo was just five and had a Great Dane called Hamlet who helped us to heal.

Until then, I send you my heart's love on all the pages of this journal, which holds only eight months worth of events but is now filled to bursting.

Your mother-to-be,
Fiona Rose Macgregor

Epilogue

✸

The first astonishing event to follow this story was the birth of Father and Aunt's son Ben, just a year after they were married. The girls were shocked, but Theo was overjoyed to have a brother at last, even if he was only a baby. He saw to it that Benjy grew up to make mischief, as he had done himself.

Jo finished her medical training but she did not marry William Galt. She stayed single and became a sought-after midwife and baby doctor. When she was thirty, she met a doctor who planned to go out to China as a medical missionary. The pair married and went to China together. They had no children, but Jo opened an orphanage and loved the children as if they were her own.

Jo's friend Carrie Galt achieved her dream and became a doctor. She also married one — a fellow medical student whom she came to know years after the flu epidemic was over.

Fanny attended the Macdonald Institute in Guelph and trained to be a dietician. She married a farmer and ended up having boy triplets.

Theo grew interested in flying and joined the Air Force at the outbreak of the Second World War. He fell in love with a British girl named Sabrina and they settled in England and had a daughter whom they called Jemma. When Jemma was two they came to Canada on a visit and, while here, Sabrina contracted polio. She was able to survive only by being in an iron lung which enabled her to breathe. She lived in the hospital, and Theo and Jemma stayed with Fee.

Father and Aunt's son, Ben, became interested in ham radio and, when he grew up, got a job as a radio announcer. He fell hopelessly in love with an actress, but she was not interested in him, so he remained a bachelor all his life.

Fee herself did write short stories for magazines, as well as two children's novels, before marrying a man who ran his family's grocery business. They had no children until Fee was nearly forty, and then she gave birth to a baby with Down's syndrome. Fee loved him dearly and insisted on keeping him at home even though, at that time, many such children were placed in institutions. The child had a badly damaged heart, however, and died when he was just five. Without her own child in the house, Fee grew increasingly closer to her niece, Jemma.

When David Macgregor and Rose were growing old, Fee and her husband and Theo and Jemma moved back into the old house on Collier Street, where they could all care for each other. Theo went back to university and eventually became a philosophy professor. Although Sabrina's paralysis could not be cured, in time it became possible for her to live outside the hospital. She was moved to Collier Street, too, where she and Fee became as close as Fee and Fanny had been.

One day, when Theo's Jemma was thirteen, Fee found her old diary and she and Jemma began reading it aloud with Sabrina listening. They all enjoyed it hugely even though Jemma cried over her Aunt Jemma's death.

Finally Jemma said, "Aunt Fee, you are just like Aunt in this book. You love us all. But you would still rather read a book than clean house." And Fee, laughing and blushing a little, admitted that Jemma had seen through her. Keeping house for such a large family would not have given her much chance to indulge in her love for reading, except that Sabrina had a nurse who came by during the day to help with her care, and Theo also paid for a daily woman who was a dedicated housecleaner and cook.

Fee marvelled, as the years passed, at how much was written about the Great War and how little was remembered of the devastating Spanish Flu that had ravaged her family. Whenever Fanny came to visit, the two of them often spoke of those days when Fanny's near death drew them so close together.

Historical Note

❀

"Have you had your flu shot yet?" we ask each other as autumn brings shorter days. "I think I must be getting the flu," we tell our families and friends. "I ache all over." We feel no fear, only irritation at the prospect of a few uncomfortable days swallowing pills, drinking juice, resting, moaning and feeling sorry for ourselves. Unless we know that we are extra frail and susceptible, we do not see "flu" as endangering our lives, although approximately 5 million Canadians get the flu each year, and up to 1500 die. We may feel truly miserable as the days pass without our being able to shake off the symptoms, yet few of us are fearful.

We have forgotten the Spanish Flu.

Yet we in Canada, at the beginning of a new century, are beginning to be reminded. Daily, we read in the paper about the Norwalk virus or the West Nile virus. We are given frequent updates on the advance of the avian flu across Asia and into Europe. On television, we have seen people walking the streets of Hong Kong wearing masks. Only a few years ago, SARS hit Toronto, killing over 40 people. Many families who may have been exposed to the disease were required to put themselves in voluntary quarantine until they were past the incubation period and safe from infection. Even after the acute danger passed, we wash our hands more frequently and more thoroughly than we did before, since we are told constantly that washing your hands often and thoroughly is one of the best ways to halt the spread of influenza. And, more and more, we are being reminded about the flu epidemic that swept across Canada and the world in 1918–1919.

Authorities are starting to think about stockpiling flu medication, and wondering whether we will be ready for the next pandemic. Politicians reassure us, but medical personnel are not so positive.

I came to understand the concern the medical profession has been feeling only after beginning to research the Spanish Flu. Here are some of the astonishing, often heart-rending, facts that I found: more people died worldwide from the Spanish Flu than combatants killed in World War I. Estimates range from 20 million to 22 million people in only a few months. Some researchers even suggest that, because deaths from the flu were not always reported fully in underdeveloped countries, millions *more* may have died of the Spanish Flu. In Canada, over 2 million people got the flu, with up to 50,000 dying from it — approximately 1 in 6 of those who contracted the flu died. (In the United States the figure was 1 in 4.) Across the country, undertakers were swamped with work. Toronto was so short on hearses to carry the dead that streetcars were used to move the bodies. In other communities, trucks were used.

But it is the human loss and human grief caused by the Spanish Flu that stand out — as well as human courage in the face of it. It is time we studied what happened in 1918 and to consider how this world of ours has changed during the years since. So much is different now, but not all the differences will help to save us from such a pandemic if it actually comes.

What is a "pandemic"? It is an epidemic which infects not just one city or even one province or state, but spreads throughout the world. Earlier such diseases were the Plague (sometimes called the Black Death) and cholera. HIV–AIDS is a pandemic that has spread across most of the globe and has killed millions of people throughout many countries, especially those in Africa.

Polio was once a terrifying illness that killed or crippled thousands of people. In the past, measles and diphtheria were also responsible for thousands of deaths. We in the western world no longer fear these last three diseases so much, because vaccines have been developed which have brought them under control. Scientists are now working night and day in an effort to develop similar vaccines to counter the flu, in all its many variants.

Why are we searching so desperately? Because all

our current "miracle drugs" cannot defeat a deadly virus much better than medicines could in 1918. We have ways of fighting viruses, ways that our ancestors lacked. But they are still not sufficient.

THE SPANISH FLU

Despite its name, the Spanish Flu did not begin in Spain. There are several theories about how the word Spanish became associated with it, one being that reports of the disease first appeared in Spanish newspapers — Spain, being neutral in World War I, was less concerned about reporting deaths than the Allied or German press were.

The first North American cases of the Spanish Flu epidemic were reported at Fort Riley, a military base in Kansas. Over 100 servicemen stationed there in March, 1918, began to show symptoms of having "colds," and within weeks over 1000 soldiers were sick enough to be sent to hospital. Some of the sick were sent home — and carried the contagion with them. Others, who had not yet developed acute symptoms or were still in the incubation stage and therefore appeared healthy, were shipped overseas to fight. The Spanish Flu travelled with both groups. The virus had already begun to appear in soldiers in Europe and the British Isles — in May of 1918 over 10,000 sailors from the British fleet were sick.

The contagion reached Canada during the summer of 1918, appearing among the civilian population in a college at Victoriaville, Quebec. Although the illness was reported in the press, nobody was unduly alarmed at first. It took longer then for people to travel from place to place — many people were born, raised and lived out their lives within a day's journey of the town where they spent their childhoods. Quebec, which seems so close to Toronto today, was not close at all to people like Fee Macgregor and her family. Yet, late in September, a little girl from Jesse Ketchum School died in the Toronto General Hospital — Toronto's first Spanish Flu fatality. Canadians, having endured a war that killed almost 60,000 of their young men, were about to experience the outbreak of a disease that would claim up to 50,000 civilians, who had believed themselves to be safe at home. Often the two groups overlapped. Some servicemen returning to Canada brought the contagion with them; some contracted it after they returned home, thinking themselves to be far from the Front and out of danger. Eighteen-year-old Alan McLeod, Canada's youngest recipient of the Victoria Cross (the Commonwealth's highest award for valour), survived the war but died from the flu soon after returning home a hero.

As the death toll from the flu mounted across the country, complacency ended. Schools were quarantined. Public meetings were cancelled. Bowling alleys closed and public libraries shut their doors to the public. Even the Stanley Cup playoffs were cancelled.

In Ontario, the government organized over 400 women to become Sisters of Service (S.O.S.). Other areas of the country launched similar appeals, and women responded. In Toronto, volunteers attended three lectures on how to help the sick, and then went to work. Besides actively nursing the desperately ill, there was a need for food to be taken to families who had nobody to prepare meals. There were thousands of gauze masks to be made and distributed. As Eileen Pettigrew explains in *The Silent Enemy: Canada and the Deadly Flu of 1918*, "Social barriers of the time were forgotten. Women who had never come closer to the mechanics of housekeeping than to instruct their cooks and chauffeurs, nursed people they didn't know, changed beds, cooked, and did laundry." Women across the country pitched in to help families where the flu had struck, at great risk to themselves.

Soon overworked hospital staff were falling ill. Telephone operators became sick, too. In 1918, every phone call was put through by a living operator working at a switchboard. The operator would ask for the number you wanted and place the call for you. With fewer operators available, the public was asked to confine phone calls to emergencies only, because otherwise the whole system would be unable to manage. Many stores closed. Since most people did not yet have cars, and those available were sometimes appropriated for official business during wartime, people had to walk farther and carry home whatever was needed — unless they had a horse or a bicycle. It was another strain on already overtaxed people. The list of services that faltered under the strain is endless.

THE FLU STRIKES

The Spanish Flu began with back pain, coughing, fever — the same symptoms we associate with flu today. Some victims experienced profuse bleeding from the nose as well. If Spanish Flu victims did not recover within a few days, their breathing problems soon became desperate as pneumonia developed, filling sufferers' lungs with phlegm or mucus and fluid. Eventually, there was no space for each new breath and people died, drowning in their own fluids. At the onset of the flu, doctors would see their patients grow flushed. If pneumonia developed, the flush darkened into a dark blue-grey. Some people even reported that their loved ones' faces turned black before they died. Spanish Influenza did not drag on for weeks and weeks, giving families false hope. Usually, for those who died, it was all over within a week or ten days.

Surprisingly, most of the people who died of the Spanish Flu were not the "usual" flu victims — frail elderly people or vulnerable children. Those did die, of course, but many Spanish Flu victims were adults between 20 and 50 years of age. This resulted in parents dying and children being suddenly orphaned.

If you ask the members of your family who know about the past, many will tell you that someone related to you died in the Spanish Flu pandemic — perhaps your great-great-grandmother or a great-great-uncle or most of a family down the street were taken. If you are ever visiting an old graveyard, check dates on the headstones to see how many people died in 1918 or 1919, and what their ages were when they died.

Not only adults died, though. Whole families perished, some almost overnight. As you read accounts of this disaster, people say, over and over again, "It was so quick. She was fine when we went to bed on Monday night and she was dead three days later."

Ironically, some people caught the Spanish Flu because they were so happy about the war ending that they rushed out into the crowds who thronged the streets of their town or city on Armistice Day, hugging and kissing each other because the Great War was over at last. Even some soldiers who had come home from the battlefields in Europe contracted the flu in exactly this way. The public had been so careful. They had stayed in quarantine. Many, especially in the western provinces where officials insisted on it, had worn masks. Everyone knew the danger. Yet, when news of the Armistice reached them, many threw caution to the wind and danced and sang and embraced each other — and some passed the infection on, literally from mouth to mouth.

In 1918, doctors had few weapons to fight with. All that could be done was to keep the afflicted person as comfortable as possible, struggle to bring down their fever with cool water and drinks, give them drugs for pain . . . and pray they would be spared.

Today we have some better methods for fighting the flu. We have flu shots — something that was unheard of when people across the world died of the Spanish Flu in 1918–1919. Vaccines can help keep us from catching the flu in the first place. There are now some antiviral drugs, which can help us get better faster. Antibiotics can help with other infections we might catch while our immune systems are battling flu. But there is still no "magic bullet" against the flu, and no guarantee that the strain of flu that hits in any year will be prevented by the vaccine.

We also know the value of taking sensible precautions, such as the simple act of washing your hands (taking time to sing "Happy Birthday" through twice while you are about it, or if you hate singing that, try "Row, Row, Row Your Boat"). And use soap — flu bugs loathe soap.

But our modern inventions have, in some ways, made us more vulnerable. Now, not only can *we* fly around the world with ease, so can each new strain of a flu virus, using us as its host.

The story of the Spanish Flu is a frightening one, but if you find it too scary, remember that we understand the causes and spread of the flu in a way families in 1918 could not. They had no radios, few telephones, no television, no Internet. Today our scientists and doctors are working to develop a vaccine to stop the avian flu in its tracks. When SARS arrived in Toronto, 44 people died, but think what a difference that is from the 1200 who perished in the city when the Spanish Flu struck. We may not live in a safe world, but we do live in one that is alert to the danger of another pandemic.

Jesse Ketchum Public School, which the author attended when she was young. Toronto's first fatality from the Spanish Flu was a little girl who also attended Jesse Ketchum.

A hospital ship carrying wounded soldiers back to Canada docks at Halifax, Nova Scotia. Unknown to some of the soldiers, they carried the flu with them.

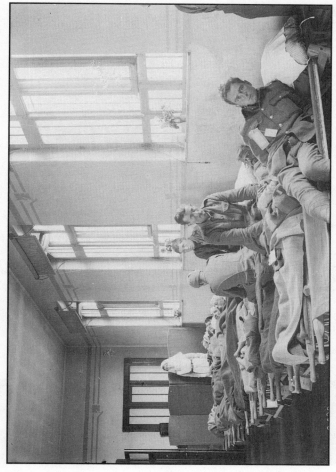

Soldiers recuperate from their injuries in a hospital ward.

ONTARIO EMERGENCY VOLUNTEER
HEALTH AUXILIARY

WANTED—VOLUNTEERS!!

The Provincial Board of Health, with the authority of the Government of Ontario, has organized an "Ontario Emergency Volunteer Health Auxiliary" for the purpose of training and supplying nursing help to be utilized wherever needed in combating the Influenza outbreak. A strong Executive has been formed in Toronto. It is recommended that each Municipal Council and Local Board of Health, working in co-operation, take immediate steps to form a local branch of this organization. The Volunteer Nurses will wear the officially authorized badge, "Ontario S.O.S." (Sisters of Service). This "S.O.S." call may be urgent. Classes taking lectures are already opened in the Parliament Buildings, Toronto (Private Bills Committee Room, ground floor), where they will be carried on every day at 10 a.m. and 3 p.m. until further notice. Young women of education are urged to avail themselves of this unique opportunity to be of real service to the community. If they are not needed, so much the better. If they are needed, we hope to have them ready. All towns and cities are urged to organize and prepare in a similar manner.

A Syllabus of Lectures is being sent to the Medical Officer of Health of all cities and towns. Further information may be had on application to John W. S. McCullough, M.D., Chairman of Executive, Parliament Buildings, Toronto, Telephone Main 5800.

C. S. NEWTON, Sec.-Treas.   W. D. McPHERSON, President.

J. W. S. McCULLOUGH, Chairman of Executive Committee.

Over 400 Toronto women responded to the call to become Sisters of Service, risking their own lives to nurse those sick with the flu.

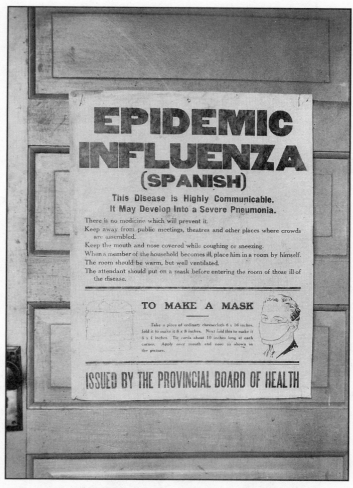

This poster was issued by the Provincial Board of Health in Alberta, to give citizens information about the influenza epidemic.

Employees of the Canadian Imperial Bank of Commerce in Calgary take extra precautions against the flu.

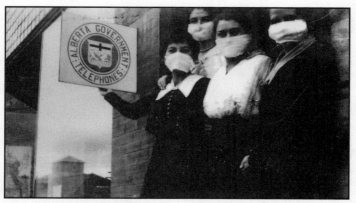

In Alberta, telephone operators (above) and prairie farmers (below) wear masks to keep the flu at bay. Masks for sale in Calgary cost between 5¢ and 25¢. In Grande Prairie, Alberta, there was a $50 fine for not wearing a mask.

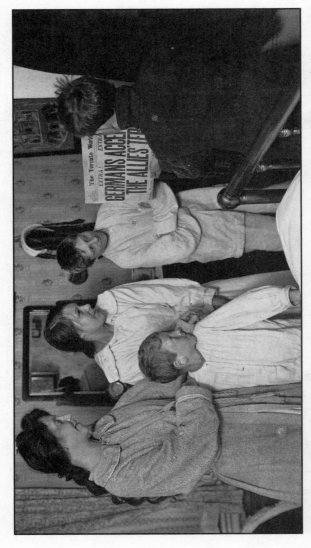

When the armistice was announced in the early hours of November 11, 1918, people just wakened from sleep pulled coats over their pyjamas and took to the streets to celebrate. The headline reads: *GERMANS ACCEPT THE ALLIES' TERMS.*

Both young and old took part in the victory celebrations.
A young girl riding on the hood of a Ford wears a soldier's
cap.

233

Over 200,000 Torontonians took to the streets to watch the Armistice Day parade. Here, some children ride the running boards of a car while adults wave Union Jacks.

This ad for a child's velocipede appeared in the 1927 Eaton's Catalogue. In a 1918 ad a similar Canuck Velocipede sold for $3.85.

235

Crossing the Bar

Sunset and evening star,
And one clear call for me!
And may there be no moaning of the bar,
When I put out to sea,
But such a tide as moving seems asleep,
Too full for sound and foam,
When that which drew from out the boundless deep
Turns again home.

Twilight and evening bell,
And after that the dark!
And may there be no sadness of farewell,
When I embark;
For tho' from out our bourne of Time and Place
The flood may bear me far,
I hope to see my Pilot face to face
When I have crost the bar.

— *Alfred, Lord Tennyson*

Requiem

Under the wide and starry sky,
Dig the grave and let me lie.
Glad did I live and gladly die,
  And I laid me down with a will.

This be the verse you grave for me:
Here he lies where he longed to be;
Home is the sailor, home from sea,
  And the hunter home from the hill.

— *Robert Louis Stevenson*

Rules for the Macgregors' Version of Pounce:

Each player has his or her own deck of Flinch cards. Use the cards numbered from 1 (ace) to 13 — no face cards or jokers. Mark the back of each card in each person's deck with a symbol such as a star or oval, so it's different from other players' decks.

After shuffling his or her deck, each player counts off 13 cards for their Pounce Pile, which they place face-down, except for the top card, which is placed face-up to their left. Then they place 4 cards face-up beside the Pounce Pile, to their right.

Play commences whenever the "chosen one" — the loser of the previous match — says "Go!"

The object of the game is to play all the cards in your Pounce Pile, as quickly as possible. You begin by going through the cards in your hand and in your Pounce Pile, counting by threes and trying to use every third card. You can add this card to any of the 4 cards beside your Pounce Pile the same way you would play Solitaire, so long as it is next in number. That is, you can place a 5 on top of a 4, a 10 on top of a 9, and so on. If you turn up an ace, it counts as a 1 and you place it in the "common area" between the players.

There is no taking turns; eveyone plays at once. All players can place a card on *all* piles, even *another* player's pile and *any* of the common piles, until the 13 is placed on any pile. Once a 13 is played on the top, that player MUST turn the pile OVER!

Once you've gone through your deck, always counting by threes, you begin again. And once your Pounce Pile is totally finished you yell "POUNCE" and all play stops IMMEDIATELY!

To score, you separate all played cards by the design on the back of the cards, and then the players count their cards (identified by the different design on the back) and the scorekeeper records the tally. (Each card counts as 1 point towards your score, whether it is an ace or a 7.) Before you begin playing, all players decide on the total that they consider a winning amount, such as 100.

The game can resemble a free-for-all as players reach across the table to slap down their cards on other players' stacks before someone else can do so. It's a fun game for anywhere from two to six players. (Jean Little herself recalls a game where twenty players were involved.)

Note: Pounce is also known as Nerts, Racing Demon, Peanuts and Squeal, and there are interesting variations in the way the games are played. An Internet search on any of these names will bring up the rules for it.

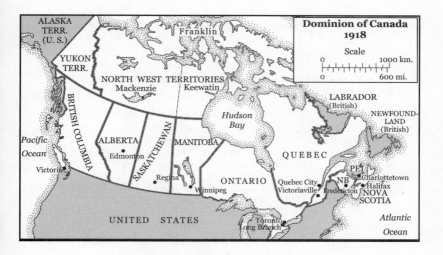

Estimated deaths from the Spanish Flu, across Canada:
British Columbia: No provincial statistics are available, but Vancouver alone had between 800–1,000 deaths
Alberta: 33,000–38,000 cases, 3,300–4,000 deaths
Saskatchewan: over 5,000 deaths
Manitoba: No provincial statistics are available, but Winnipeg reported between 820–1,020 deaths
Northwest Territories: No statistics are available
Ontario: 300,000 cases, 8,705 recorded deaths
Quebec: 535,700 cases, 13,880 deaths
New Brunswick: 35,581 cases, 1,394 deaths
Prince Edward Island: 101 deaths
Nova Scotia: 1,600 deaths
Newfoundland and Labrador: No firm statistics are available, but more than a third of the people along the Labrador coast died.

Though the number of deaths totalled up to 50,000 in Canada, that was still less than half of one percent of the population. In the United States, the Spanish Flu killed an estimated 500,000–700,000 people.

Acknowledgments

Grateful acknowledgment is made for permission to reprint the following:

Cover portrait: Detail (colourized) from black and white photo, Waldren Studios Collection, Box 54, File 103, Dalhousie University Archives/image 40_098.
Cover background: Detail (tinted) from Special Hospital Ward, Long Branch, Ont., 1918, Library and Archives Canada/PA-022917.

Page 225: Old Jesse Ketchum School (Toronto, c. 1875) by Bernard Gloster, Toronto Public Library, T 12224, slide MTL 1472.
Page 226: Hospital ship docking at Halifax, N.S., June 29, 1917, Library and Archives Canada, PA-023007.
Page 227: Casualties just arrived. No. 1 Casualty Clearing Station. July, 1916, Library and Archives Canada, PA-000324.
Page 228: Ad from *The Toronto Daily Star,* p. 20, October 15, 1918, Toronto Public Library.
Page 229: Poster issued by the Provincial Board of Health, Glenbow Museum, NA-4548-5.
Page 230: CIBC employees in Calgary, Alberta, Glenbow Museum, NA-964-22.
Page 231 (upper): Telephone operators wearing masks, Glenbow Museum, NA-3452-2.
Page 231 (lower): Men wearing masks during the Spanish influenza epidemic, Library and Archives Canada, PA-025025.
Page 232: A Family Reads Armistice Day Headlines, City of Toronto Archives, Fonds 1244, Item 892.
Page 233: Armistice Day Celebrations, City of Toronto Archives, Fonds 1244, Item 905.
Page 234: Armistice Day, Bay and King Streets, City of Toronto Archives, Fonds 1244, Item 891.
Page 235: Ad from the 1927 Eaton's Catalogue.
Pages 237–238: Rules for Pounce courtesy of Robin Little.

Page 239: Map by Paul Heersink/Paperglyphs. Map data © 2002 Government of Canada with permission from Natural Resources Canada.

*This story is dedicated to Sandra Bogart Johnston,
the editor of the Dear Canada books,
who talked me into writing one
and took me safely through the process —
even making it fun —
with much love from Victoria, Eliza, Fee and me.*

*I would like to thank the staff at the Guelph
Public Library, Barbara Hehner, and
Dr. Heather MacDougall of the University of
Waterloo, who checked my facts and answered
my questions and helped me find out all the things
I needed to know to write this book. Without you,
I would have been lost indeed. I would also like
to thank my mother, Gorrie Gauld, for keeping
a diary during her first year in medical school
in 1918. They all helped and inspired me.
All the glaring errors remaining are my own.*

241

About the Author

Jean Little draws memories, family tales and anecdotes from every imaginable source to create her heartwarming stories. Her mother, Gorrie Gauld, was a sixteen-year-old medical student in 1918, so Jean was able to sift through Gorrie's diaries from 1918–1919 in writing the story of the Macgregor family. Jean's younger brother's bout with pneumonia in 1940 also made its way into this book — she recalls complaining about Hugh's loud "snoring," only to have her parents discover that he had pneumonia!

The lively card game of Pounce is a Little family favourite, and Jean weaves in bits from her own schoolgirl days at Toronto's Jesse Ketchum Public School, which she attended after coming to Canada with her medical missionary parents in 1939.

One of Jean's close friends, Loa Reuber, lost her mother to the Spanish Flu. On her third birthday, Loa was not having a birthday party, but attending her mother's funeral: "Her brothers and sisters stayed with their father after her mother's death," Jean says, "but, because she was just three, Loa was sent to live with her grandparents. She was given a doll on that birthday, one that her mother had dressed for her; but although Loa took great care of the doll, she never felt comfortable playing with it."

Jean makes many visits to schools to talk about her books. Legally blind since birth, she is always accompanied by her guide dog, Honey, who came to Jean in 2006 after her previous guide dog, Pippa, retired. Pippa still lives in the Little household, along with a bird, three other dogs, two cats and two turtles.

Orphan at My Door, Jean Little's first book in the Dear Canada series, won the Canadian Library Association Book of the Year Award in 2002. *Brothers Far from Home* is a CLA Honour Book.

Jean has written over forty books, including novels, picture books, a book of short stories, poetry and two autobiographies — *Stars Come Out Within* and *Little by Little*. Books such as *Pippin the Christmas Pig, Mama's Going to Buy You a Mockingbird, Listen for the Singing, Mine for Keeps, From Anna, His Banner Over Me, Willow and Twig* and *Hey World, Here I Am!* have won her many awards, including the Ruth Schwartz Award, the Canada Council Children's Literature Prize, the Violet Downey Award, the Little, Brown Canadian Children's Book Award, the Boston Globe–Horn Book Honor Book Award and the Mr. Christie's Book Award. Jean received the Vicky Metcalf Award in 1974 for her Body of Work, and is a member of the Order of Canada. Her newest picture book, with illustrator Werner Zimmermann, is *Listen, Said the Donkey*.

Library and Archives Canada Cataloguing in Publication

Little, Jean, 1932-
If I die before I wake : the flu epidemic diary of Fiona Macgregor /
Jean Little.

(Dear Canada)
ISBN-13: 978-0-439-98837-7
ISBN-10: 0-439-98837-3

1. Influenza Epidemic, 1918-1919--Canada--Juvenile fiction.   2. World
War, 1914-1918--Canada--Juvenile fiction.   I. Title.   II. Series.
PS8523.I77I32 2007   jC813'.54   C2006-904964-5

❊

6 5 4 3 2 1   Printed in Canada   07 08 09 10 11

❊

The display type was set in Galahad.
The text was set in Galliard.

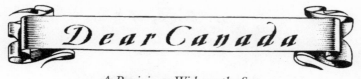

Dear Canada

A Prairie as Wide as the Sea
The Immigrant Diary of Ivy Weatherall
by Sarah Ellis

Orphan at My Door
The Home Child Diary of Victoria Cope
by Jean Little

With Nothing But Our Courage
The Loyalist Diary of Mary MacDonald
by Karleen Bradford

Footsteps in the Snow
The Red River Diary of Isobel Scott
by Carol Matas

A Ribbon of Shining Steel
The Railway Diary of Kate Cameron
by Julie Lawson

Whispers of War
The War of 1812 Diary of Susanna Merritt
by Kit Pearson

Alone in an Untamed Land
The Filles du Roi *Diary of Hélène St. Onge*
by Maxine Trottier

Brothers Far from Home
The World War I Diary of Eliza Bates
by Jean Little

An Ocean Apart
The Gold Mountain Diary of Chin Mei-ling
by Gillian Chan

Banished from Our Home
The Acadian Diary of Angélique Richard
by Sharon Stewart

A Trail of Broken Dreams
The Gold Rush Diary of Harriet Palmer
by Barbara Haworth-Attard

Winter of Peril
The Newfoundland Diary of Sophie Loveridge
by Jan Andrews

Turned Away
The World War II Diary of Devorah Bernstein
by Carol Matas

The Death of My Country
The Plains of Abraham Diary of Geneviève Aubuchon
by Maxine Trottier

No Safe Harbour
The Halifax Explosion Diary of Charlotte Blackburn
by Julie Lawson

A Rebel's Daughter
The 1837 Rebellion Diary of Arabella Stevenson
by Janet Lunn

A Season for Miracles
Twelve Tales of Christmas